Kildare Librar Arts Service
Seirbhís Le   ̱ Chill

Tp

THE PARADISE GARDEN

THE PARADISE GARDEN

Christina Green

CHIVERS

THORNDIKE

This Large Print edition is published by BBC Audiobooks Ltd, Bath, England and by Thorndike Press®, Waterville, Maine, USA.

Published in 2003 in the U.K. by arrangement with the author.

Published in 2003 in the U.S. by arrangement with Dorian Literary Agency.

U.K. Hardcover   ISBN 0–7540–7370–X (Chivers Large Print)
U.K. Softcover   ISBN 0–7540–7371–8 (Camden Large Print)
U.S. Softcover   ISBN 0–7862–5773–3 (Nightingale)

Copyright © Christina Green, 2003

The text of this Large Print edition is unabridged.
Other aspects of the book may vary from the original edition.

Set in 16 pt. New Times Roman.

Printed in Great Britain on acid-free paper.

British Library Cataloguing in Publication Data available

Library of Congress Cataloging-in-Publication Data

Green, Christina.
        The paradise garden / by Christina Green.
            p.   cm.
        ISBN 0–7862–5773–3 (lg. print : sc : alk. paper)
        1. Large type books. I. Title.
    PR6057.R3378P37 2003
    823'.914—dc21   2003053356

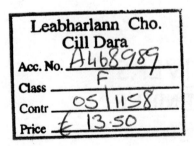

CHAPTER ONE

Daphne Chandler sat upright in her nursing-home bed and looked across the room to where Mel sat by the window.

'Melanie,' she said urgently, 'I want you to look after my garden.'

For a moment Mel was silent. Of all the favours Daphne might ask, this was one she hadn't anticipated.

'Good heavens, Daphne,' she said, startled, 'but I don't know a thing about gardening.'

'You could learn.'

The old lady's voice was very firm despite the heart condition which had brought her into Grange Nursing Home a few weeks before.

'And I could trust you to do it properly. You know what my garden means to me.'

'Yes, of course, but honestly, I don't think . . . I mean, I'm so busy as it is. Becky and I are working long hours at our catering business, Daphne. Where would I find the time?'

Daphne looked at her young friend with a steady gaze.

'If you value our friendship,' she said quietly, 'I know you would find an hour or two each week to try and keep my garden at least looking tidy.'

'Of course I value our friendship!' Mel said heatedly. 'You know that! You were so good to me when Andrew left, when I felt so lonely and disappointed, and when we started the home catering you supported me wonderfully. Daphne, I would really like to be able to help you, but . . .'

She fell silent, remembering. Daphne Chandler had been like a grandmother to her when she and Andrew parted. With no near relations of her own, she had relied on her old friend for positive support and loving advice. And now? Of course she must do what Daphne asked, inexperienced and busily occupied as she was.

So she smiled into the unblinking grey eyes watching her so closely from the bed and said, 'If you promise to tell me just what to do, then of course I'll do it. But don't expect it to look quite the same as your famous paradise garden, will you?'

Daphne's expression of relief was her reward and at once she knew she would somehow find time in her busy life to keep her word, but it wouldn't be easy.

She said jokily, 'You'll have to give me very detailed instructions! I'm not sure I know a primrose from a potato.'

The old lady leaned towards the bed table and pulled a large album on to her lap.

'These pictures will help, Melanie. They're the photos you took last year when those television people came and made a film about the garden.'

'And called it *The Paradise Garden*. I remember. What a day that was!'

She knew she would never forget. Indeed, the whole village would always remember the day when the television camera team took over Daphne's garden, full of June roses, lupins, delphiniums, lavender hedges, clumps of scarlet poppies and borders glowing with fragrant, old-fashioned pinks. Daphne smiled as she opened the photo album.

'Just look at those pink China roses, cascading down the wall! And there are the foxgloves and columbines growing up between the shrub roses.'

'And here's one of you, Daphne! All dressed up and sitting on your bench beneath the honeysuckle bower.'

Together they studied the photos. Mel remembered how hard Daphne had worked in the days leading up to the visit of the TV team, tying up rebellious plants, mowing the front lawn and trimming the edges until everything looked manicured and elegant. And what a job it had been on the great day, persuading Daphne to put on her best dress and the lovely straw hat trimmed with field daisies. Pleasure grew, as she remembered.

Daphne had a special memory, too.

'Here's one of the tea you and Becky provided. Your first commission, wasn't it? Devonshire splits and cream.'

'Your homemade raspberry jam, too.'

3

'And that excellent lemon-curd sponge cake that Becky made. A really wonderful meal.'

Daphne's eyes shone.

'I seem to remember everything was eaten by the time all those young men and women had tucked in!'

'Yes,' Mel said, thoughtfully. 'And after it was written up in the local paper Becky and I got masses of enquiries, which is why the business is doing so well now. Seems people just can't get enough of our Devon farm meals supplied to their tables, and cleared away afterwards! Definitely a day to remember, Daphne.'

'And now you understand, Melanie, my dear, why I can't bear the thought of my beloved garden going to rack and ruin.'

Mel nodded, but tried a last suggestion.

'I could ask around the village. Probably someone would take it on.'

'Certainly not!'

Daphne's usually gentle voice was loud and almost strident.

Mel saw the colour surging into her pale cheeks and said at once, 'No, of course not! Don't worry, Daphne, I'll do the best I can.'

They looked at each other for a moment, and Mel felt the rapport between them strengthen. She looked at Daphne fondly.

'A few hours' gardening each week is the least I can do for you, Daphne. You've always been so good to me.'

4

Daphne leaned back against her pillows and nodded.

'You and I are alike, Melanie, in having no family. I'm glad I was able to help a little when Andrew left you.'

'When we finally decided that all we felt for each other was friendship, not the great passion we'd hoped for, we'd already started living separate lives, so it was better that we split up.'

Mel laughed, but only to cover up the unhappiness she still felt.

'And anyway, I've decided that great passion isn't for me! I'll settle for independence.'

'And how do you feel about it now, my dear? Nearly two years ago, I believe?'

Mel nodded.

'I'm still lonely at times, of course, but I've got the business to keep me occupied and Becky and I are very close friends. Sometimes I take young Susi off her hands for an hour or so. Susi's a bit of a handful and Becky's so busy with the cooking, you see.'

'While you deal with the administration, I suppose?'

'Yes. I do the shopping, deal with new clients, new recipes, all the money matters. It all takes time.'

'And now you're going to find time for my poor garden, as well. Melanie, I really am extremely grateful. If only I had a family, I wouldn't have to ask you, but there's only

James, my nephew, left.'

Her voice trailed away and she looked at Mel with wry amusement.

'The black sheep, if ever there was one! James and I never got along, I fear. A horrid little boy. He used to trap grasshoppers in a jam jar and then forget them. And then there was the question of the money, but I won't go into that.'

Mel watched her jaw tighten as she went on.

'Enough to say that James is never going to be allowed into either Glebe Cottage or its garden. So that's why I have to impose on you, my dear.'

They smiled at each other and as Daphne leaned back, the photo album slipped to the floor. Mel bent and picked it up, putting it back on the bed. It opened at the beginning of the book and for a moment they both looked down at the first page, which was unexpectedly empty. Mel saw old-fashioned corner stickers which had obviously once secured a large photograph.

'You must have lost this one,' she said casually. 'Was it important?'

To her consternation, Daphne gasped and clutched at the album, her heavily-veined hands clawing as if at some priceless treasure. She said nothing, but her face was suddenly a picture of desperation. For a moment she had trouble in catching her breath and Mel was about to ring for a nurse when gradually

Daphne regained self-control. Her hands stopped shaking and she closed her eyes for a few seconds, and then, opening them, met Mel's anxious gaze.

'It's all right,' she managed slowly, her voice weak and only just audible. 'Nothing to worry about. Just a shock, that was all.'

Mel held her hand and waited for the shallow breathing to settle. She closed the album, putting it on the bed table and wondering exactly what had caused Daphne to react in such an alarming way, over a missing photo. Surely it wasn't enough to bring about such a shock, such desperation on her face, in her eyes. But Mel knew it would be better to ignore it and help Daphne to recover.

Soothingly, she said, 'I expect you've had too much excitement, Daphne, worrying about the garden. A nap would do you good, and anyway, it's time for me to go. I promised I'd fetch Susi after school as Becky's got a big menu to cook today. Susi would only get under her feet.'

Daphne was already looking better. She smiled weakly.

'You're very good to Becky. Single mothers need all the help they can get. Yes, you must go now, Melanie, my dear. But come again soon. You're always welcome, you know.'

Mel kissed the lined forehead and put her chair back against the wall.

'I'll go and have a look at your garden after

7

I've picked up Susi and then I'll come in tomorrow and report to you.'

She tried to jolly things along and give Daphne something to smile about as she left.

'So you'd better start making a list of instructions for me!'

Her voice was very positive, but she wasn't sure that she could make the neglected garden live up to its famous name. She was relieved to see Daphne's warm smile returning, but then felt the old sting of anxiety as the soft voice spoke thoughtfully.

'Of course, it'll only be for a short time, Melanie, just until I can get back to Glebe Cottage and see to the garden myself.'

Mel left the room, thinking about the doctor's report on Daphne.

'Miss Chandler needs rest and good nutrition and no strenuous exercise. We'll see how she gets on, but I don't really think she'll be going home in the near future.'

Did Daphne know this? She knew the garden would never be the same without its owner's knowledge and tender loving care, but she made a vow to herself to do the very best she could.

She reached the entrance at the same time as the door opened and a tall, large man, who seemed to fill the whole doorway, almost bumped into her. They apologised at the same time, which led to an exchange of smiles. Then the man stood aside.

'Do you know which room Miss Chandler is in?' he asked.

'Yes,' Mel said. 'Number five, along this passage and first on the left. And there's a nurse in the office just before you get there.'

She paused uncertainly.

'Is Miss Chandler expecting you?'

He looked down at her from his six foot plus height and smiled.

'Yes. She wrote, asking me to call.'

It was a low, husky voice, curiously attractive. Unusual sea-green eyes looked directly into hers and Mel at once felt he must think her unnecessarily curious. But she also had the strangest feeling that this man, with his thick, fair hair and worn, leather jacket somehow had the knack of understanding the thoughts behind words. It was a new, unwanted feeling, because, since Andrew left, she had promised herself never again to look at a man with any sense of attraction. She couldn't bear to run the risk of all that unhappiness again. But, yes, this man with the perceptive gaze, was definitely appealing.

With a feeling of defiance she lifted her chin, saying quickly, 'Just don't tire her, will you?' and then she turned, leaving him standing by the door.

Easy to forget the casual encounter, she decided, yet she felt his eyes on her all the way to her parked car outside. She couldn't stop thinking about him as she drove through the village towards the school. Mid-thirties, she guessed and then wondered, smiling wryly, what he and Daphne could have in common—Daphne with her old-fashioned, dignified style of life and this guy with his distressed jeans and open-necked shirt. The images were strong, and stayed in her mind as she drove on.

She thought, too, about Daphne's past life which seemed to be becoming increasingly full of mysteries. Why had she never married? Long ago, Daphne had admitted to loving children and would have made a good mother. And there was that photograph of a young, handsome man in her bedroom, all part of the mystery, as was her shock over the missing photo in the album. Perhaps the youthful Daphne had decided independence was more attractive than marriage and its restraints. But Mel knew her old friend was unlikely to reveal anything of her past life.

Susi jumped in the car as soon as she parked outside the school.

'Hi, Mel!'

With her bright, speedwell blue eyes and ceaseless energy, Susi was certainly a handful. Becky, always busy with the mixing bowl, was grateful for the help Mel gave in helping to cope with the five-year-old. Mel enjoyed Susi's company, exhausting though it was.

She had once hoped to have a family, but not only had her view of marriage changed, she had pushed away that once-urgent need.

She told herself defiantly, who needed men? Like Daphne, Mel valued her independence. She was a career girl and she wouldn't let maudlin thoughts change anything. But it was nice to have Susi for company sometimes. If living alone had many advantages it also contained the threat of loneliness.

'Hi, Susi,' she said brightly. 'I'm going to ring your mum and tell her we won't be going straight home.'

She punched Becky's number and grinned at the child as it rang.

'Why not? Where're we going?'

'To Miss Chandler's paradise garden. Hi, Becky.'

Becky agreed and Mel told Susi her mum was happy for her to be a bit late home, and then drove through the quiet, country village, towards the grey-stoned towered church, parking outside nearby Glebe Cottage.

The famous paradise garden looked a mess. Now, in mid-summer, all the freshness was over. The once spectacular flower beds had turned into a tangle of overcrowded seedheads and domineering weeds. The paradise garden had turned into a wilderness.

Susi stared as they slowly walked up the gravel path from the gate.

'Who's going to make it better?' she asked, and Mel smiled wryly.

'Me,' she said, and then added spontaneously, 'and you.'

11

What a good idea! If she and Susi came for an hour, say three afternoons a week, surely they could tame this jungle between them.

'What do you say, Susi? Will you help me clear up this muddle and make it a proper garden again?'

Susi didn't hesitate, and jumping up and down in excitement, she burst out with, 'Yes! Shall we start now?'

Mel laughed.

'Not right this minute. I've got work waiting for me at home and your mum's expecting you for tea. We'll come tomorrow after school. How about it?'

Susi pulled a disappointed face. Then suddenly she swooped down the path and kneeled by a crowded flower bed.

'I'll pick some of these for Miss Chandler.'

Mel looked at the golden heads that the child was picking and hid her smile. Well, perhaps dandelions in full flower would be more promising a gift than dead geraniums and seeding daisies.

'Great,' she said enthusiastically. 'Take them home and put them in water and then tomorrow, after we've spent an hour here, we'll pop in to see Miss Chandler and you can give them to her. Now, I think we'd better be on our way.'

It took another five minutes to persuade Susi to leave the garden, during which time Mel wandered the paths, looking at empty

12

Glebe Cottage and wondering sadly what would happen to it once Daphne realised she wasn't returning home. Perhaps her nephew, James Chandler, who, she supposed, must be Daphne's next of kin and was also her solicitor, would deal with the problem. After all, he was the only family, so all responsibility must be his.

Mel had heard village gossip about James and wondered if a sophisticated man with his social reputation would want this once beautiful house, now in need of much upgrading inside. Unlikely, so after Daphne had gone it would be sold and someone else would take on the beautiful old place. It was a sad thought, and Mel drove home in silence, only half listening to Susi's chatter.

'We'll have to work hard, won't we? I think we need to use some magic to make it better, to make it a proper paradise garden again. You know, Mel, magic, like in fairy tales.'

Mel nodded.

'I think hard work will probably be the best bet, Susi, but, sure, work some magic if you like.'

Susi cuddled into her seat and shut her eyes.

'I shall ask the flower fairies to help. They're full of magic,' she said as the car drew up outside Becky's house.

'You do that, love, what a good idea. Out you get, now,' she said, undoing Susi's seatbelt. 'And here're your dandelions. Look after

13

them. Tell Mum I'll collect you from school tomorrow, and then we'll do a spot of work in the garden. OK, Susi?'

Mel drove home, deep in thought. Her life was already hectically busy, and now she'd promised to restore Daphne's garden! She must be mad. But, with a sudden burst of energy, she knew she'd do the very best she could, with Susi's help, of course, and perhaps just a touch of magic! As she drove down a side lane, overhung with huge oak trees, finally parking the car outside big, old high-roofed Dunmore House, where she rented the top flat, she was smiling again. Life was certainly full of surprises.

Another surprise revealed itself that very evening. Sitting down with a glass of white wine by her window overlooking the garden, Mel heard a car crunch over the gravel and park beside the hedge. She peered through the window. Who could it be? She put down her glass and edged forward to get a better view. A large man got out of the shabby-looking car and stood for a moment, looking up at the house.

Mel drew back quickly. It was the man she'd seen at the nursing home. Had he come with a message from Daphne? She stationed herself at the side of the window and continued watching, pushing aside the guilty sense of snooping. The man was bending over the open boot of the car. Obviously, he hadn't come just to see her. He pulled out a couple of bags and then wrestled with a huge box. Slowly, arms full, the luggage left beside the car, he approached the front door. Mel couldn't see any more so had to be content with imagining and listening. She could only think that he was a new tenant for the unoccupied ground-floor rooms.

At first, all was quiet, but then distant footsteps made their way through the hall below. She was intrigued and started working out what sort of a man he was—hardly a businessman, not in that weathered, leather jacket and what looked like walking boots. There he was again, returning to lock the car and collect the luggage and a pile of books. She heard a door downstairs shut and then silence.

Finishing her wine, she grinned at her own curiosity. Well, they were bound to meet, both using the same hall and front door, so she'd get to know a bit more about him. Then she chided herself. Why was she so interested in this stranger? Apart from the fact that he had visited Daphne, he meant nothing at all to her.

No more men, she'd said very firmly after Andrew had gone. She'd kept to that since then, so why change her mind now? Firmly, she switched on the TV, but found it hard to keep her mind on the figures on the screen. Her thoughts kept straying downstairs.

In the morning, she raced through some

15

invoices and a letter to a new client, suggesting alternative menus for a forthcoming christening party, and then phoned Becky.

'Hi, Becky, got your list ready? I'm just off to Sainsbury's.'

A lengthy list followed which Mel jotted down, and then Becky said, 'Susi's all ready for your gardening stint. Got her trowel and those dandelions at school with her.'

Mel laughed.

'Spade and secateurs are more like, but that'll be my department. I promised Daphne we'd do what we can, but it's a huge job.'

'Why can't James Chandler take it over? You don't know anything about gardening, do you?'

'No, and I don't imagine he does, either. He's not exactly the flavour of Daphne's month, you know. I suppose he'll be selling the cottage eventually.'

'Nasty chap, if all the gossip is right, smarmy. I don't blame Daphne for disowning him. Poor chap, sounds as if no-one wants him! Even I'm not exactly attracted, and you know I'm always on the look out!'

Becky laughed and Mel joined in. But then, unexpectedly, she found herself telling Becky about the new man downstairs.

Becky giggled and said, 'Sounds dishy,' and then added warningly, 'Now look, Mel, don't get all of a dither about him. Remember your slogan. *Who needs men? I don't!* If that's what

16

you really feel, just keep to it, girl!'

'Of course I shall.'

Mel decided to end this slightly dangerous conversation.

'OK, I'm on my way into town now. I'll bring the groceries when I return Susi after tea. Cheers, Becky.'

Collecting her purse, she looked longer than usual at the reflection in her bedroom mirror. Not a bad figure for someone approaching the dreaded thirty watershed, she supposed. She had Mum's high cheekbones, but Dad's larger than wanted mouth. She tucked the fair glossy hair behind her ear and wished she looked more impressive. But only for a moment. No need to impress anyone these days, was there?

Going downstairs, she didn't do the usual rush down the elegant mahogany staircase, and actually paused as she opened the front door to glance, without meaning to, of course, at the door opening into the ground-floor flat conversion. No sound was coming from it. Was the fair-haired guy there? Why was he here? Didn't he have a proper home of his own?

Then she cleared her mind and strode out to the waiting car, reversing out of the garden in a hurry.

The day sped past and by the time Mel parked outside the village school she felt ready to take a shower and relax, but the garden waited, and so did Susi! She brandished her trowel in one hand, and the bunch of

17

dandelions in the other as she charged out of the playground and into the car.

'I'm ready,' she told Mel gleefully. 'Are you ready, Mel?'

'Of course. Must get cracking, mustn't we?'

They were soon there, inside the gate, and Mel knew yet again that paradise had been the right description for this once-lovely jungle of flowers and bushes, and her resolve to return the wilderness to Daphne's standard strengthened. Unlocking the door of the garden shed, she sorted out tools. She found a kneeler for Susi so that she could dig up the weeds in the front of the border and a bucket to put them in, secateurs for herself and a big sunhat hanging on the inside of the creaky door.

As she settled Susi to work, she glanced at the cottage. Cobwebs and a tide of dead leaves and dirt edged the bottom of the front door. She walked around the back and peered in at the kitchen, dark, empty and very sad. It was a good thing Daphne couldn't see it.

Then Mel saw something—the drifting sunlight shining on a silver pen lying on the kitchen table, beside an opened notebook. It wasn't Daphne's pen, Mel knew. She tensed. An intruder? But there was no sign of a break-in. Then she relaxed. Probably James Chandler had been to look at the property. From all she'd heard, he wasn't one to let the grass grow under his feet. But, recalling

Daphne's firm words, how had he got in? She went back and joined Susi. They worked hard for nearly an hour and then Susi got restless.

'I'm thirsty. I'm hungry. I want my tea. Let's go home, Mel.' Mel was only too glad to agree.

'Right. But we're going to pop in and see Miss Chandler on the way.' They found Daphne sitting up in bed, her face paler than on the last visit, but her smile, as they entered, redeeming all Mel's anxieties.

'How lovely to see you, Melanie, and who is this?' Susi stepped forward and held out the flowers.

'I'm Susi Welling, I'm five and three quarters and I picked these for you in your garden.'

The flowers were deposited on Daphne's bed.

'Shall I put them in water? They'll die if I don't.'

Daphne raised the little bunch to her nose and sniffed.

'How kind of you, Susi. There's a glass over there.'

She pointed to the bed table and Susi carefully arranged them in the tumbler standing on it.

'Now,' Daphne went on, 'sit down, child, and let me tell you about the dandelions I used to pick.'

Susi, wide-eyed, sat herself on the bed next to Mel.

'Yes?'

Mel was intrigued. Surely Daphne had other things to discuss than dandelions? But instead Daphne was telling Susi about her garden.

'It's a picture,' she said proudly, 'full of beautiful, old-fashioned flowers. I can see them now—lupins, daisies, delphiniums, love-in-the-mist, those bright yellow and orange blanket flowers, violets, primroses, snowdrops in the winter. It's a real paradise garden, a place where I can sit and think, and find peace of mind.'

'And dandelions?' Susi asked anxiously, and Daphne smiled.

'Of course. I use them for my salads and to keep my blood pure, and to look lovely in a jam jar on the kitchen table when I do my cooking.'

The old woman and the child looked at each other with what Mel realised was complete understanding, and suddenly she thought how pleased she was that she'd decided to involve Susi in this problem of Daphne's garden.

'Susi, tell Miss Chandler what we've been doing today, you and your trowel, and me and the secateurs,' she said quickly.

'I've been weeding,' Susi said importantly, 'and Mel has cut the dead heads off the roses on the walls. Tomorrow we're going to collect seeds from those big orange flowers beneath the kitchen window, and later on we'll tidy up the herb bed. It's a mess, but it smells lovely, full of mint and . . . what's it called?'

'Thyme,' Daphne said gently, 'and there's parsley, and even some tarragon. That's the dragon plant.'

'Dragon!' Susi gasped. 'I'll look for it tomorrow.'

'You're working very hard, Susi, and I'm extremely grateful.'

Daphne's soft voice was alive with feeling and Mel knew that all her unwillingness to have to fit gardening into her full life had gone. Seeing Daphne's pleasure, she knew she would go on until the wilderness was really and truly a paradise garden again.

'It'll soon be better,' Susi told Daphne very firmly. 'Mel and me and the magic will make it better.'

'Magic?' Daphne mused, and exchanged glances with Mel. 'So it needs a little magic, does it, Melanie? As bad as that?'

Mel grasped the nettle.

'It's been neglected for a long time, Daphne,' she admitted, 'but we'll get it back to shape between us.'

She held her breath, watching the thoughtful, old face clear slowly and eventually smile again.

'I'm grateful,' Daphne said simply. 'Thank you, both. Now, Melanie, I want to tell you about my new friend, Stephen Summers.'

Mel's head spun.

21

'Is he the man I met yesterday, on his way to see you?'

Daphne nodded. 'Yes. He's doing a little job for me. And because he's unmarried at the moment and doesn't have a permanent home, I suggested he rent a property in the village for the next few months. I understand he's planning to move into Dunmore House.'

Carefully, Mel said, 'Yes, he did so, last night. I saw him arrive.'

'So you'll be neighbours for a while. I hope you'll help him settle in, Melanie. And perhaps even offer him a meal. The poor man is completely undomesticated, I believe.'

Mel couldn't quite believe what she was hearing. Was Daphne matchmaking?

'I'll do what I can,' she said reluctantly.

This was all she needed! A potential suitor downstairs! No thank you!

Susi was pulling at her sleeve, mouthing silently, 'I'm hungry,' and Mel at once got up.

'Sorry, Daphne, we must be on our way. Teatime, you see.'

They said their goodbyes with Susi promising to look for the dragon plant and get the magic going for Daphne.

'Next time I'll bring you some different flowers,' she promised.

'I shall look forward to that,' Daphne said, her face alight.

Mel left, thinking yet again how sad it was that Daphne's bond with children had never

22

come to fruition. She would make sure that Susi kept visiting her.

CHAPTER TWO

As Melanie began to climb the stairs to her flat, the door downstairs opened and the guy with fair hair looked up at her. His gaze and smile sent prickles down her spine.

'Hi,' he said. 'I'm your new neighbour, Stephen Summers. I've just moved in.'

Mel stopped, staring through the banisters.

'I'm Melanie Brooks. I saw you at the Grange yesterday, didn't I?'

He nodded.

'When I went to see Miss Chandler. I remember. Hard to forget.'

And then, before she could gather her shattered self-control to reply, he held out a small jug.

'No milk. Got all the other bits at the village shop, but forgot the milk. I must be the most forgetful guy in the universe. Could you help me out?'

'Of course. Come on up,' Mel heard herself saying and then watched him shut his door.

Together they climbed the stairs and she knew an urgent, unexpected regret that she was wearing jeans and yesterday's shirt instead of something sleek and more flattering. Then, as she unlocked her door and led him into the sitting-room, she silently chided herself for such ridiculous thoughts. Firmly she concentrated on being just casually social to the new neighbour. After all, Daphne had asked her to do so.

'Sit down,' she invited. 'Would you like a drink? Tea or something stronger? I've got some wine in the fridge.'

Standing still, looking out of the window at the sun-shadowed garden below, he turned, saying over his shoulder, 'Wine would be great, thanks.'

Her heart leaped uncomfortably as she went into the kitchen, but she had herself under self-control by the time she returned and gave him one of the glasses she carried.

Mel looked at Stephen sitting opposite her by the window, his hair burnished by the shaft of sunlight that slowly lit up the whole of her spacious, elegant living-room. A large, slightly untidy man, he carried with him an attractive air of being at one with the world. She took in the worn black leather jacket, the palely checked shirt and workday jeans, and wondered wryly what Daphne's reactions had been to such a state of informal dress.

He seemed relaxed, and her curiosity grew and with it a hint of enjoyment. Such relaxation was, in a way, a compliment, wasn't it? He smiled at her and his lips twitched.

'A penny for them.'

Mel felt herself colour. She sat up straighter, twitched the curtain to blot out the sunlight, and said rapidly, pushing away the traitorous thoughts, 'Well, thinking about Daphne's garden, actually. Have you seen it?'

He stretched exceedingly long legs.

'It's on my list.'

She grabbed at the straw.

'So you have a list of things to do for Daphne?'

'You're a curious girl, aren't you?'

The pale sea-green eyes twinkled and she realised she was being teased. It was a new and not entirely unpleasant feeling.

'Most women are. So tell me.'

'Just a few jobs she wants done. I'll be getting down to them tomorrow.'

Silence fell and Mel waited in vain. She tried once more.

'But I imagine her nephew, James, will be handling the business of the cottage and her finances.'

The words trailed off. She was being far too nosey. If Daphne wanted her to know anything about James and this rather mysterious Stephen then doubtless she would be informed. Until then, clearly, she must just concentrate on the garden project. But now she felt a bit resentful. She'd asked Stephen into her home, which clearly he was enjoying, she was quite ready to let him have a jug of milk, and now he wouldn't talk. Men, she thought, vengefully, and took a long sip of her wine.

'This is a lovely house,' Stephen said suddenly, staring out of the window. 'A shame to cut it in half. Have you been here long?'

'Four or five years.'

Don't tell him anything about Andrew, nothing about the business, nothing about yourself, she thought.

'Are you alone?'

'I—oh—yes.'

Really, he was too much! She clamped her lips together and got up quickly.

'I'll fetch your milk,' she called from the kitchen.

That would teach him, but it seemed Stephen Summers was unteachable. Suddenly he stood beside her at the fridge.

'This is great,' he said, nodding as he took in the efficient, state-of-the-art cooking facilities.

'You've got style, Melanie Brooks. I guess your cooking is the same.'

Again, that flash of vivid smile. His deep voice was pleasant to hear, and held a warmth that instantly banished her annoyance.

'I certainly hope so,' she said, closing the door and facing him. 'You must come and sample it sometime.'

She could have kicked herself! Why on earth, just because he had charm enough to make sparrows fall from the trees, and obviously couldn't even boil himself an egg, had she given such a stupid invitation? What had Daphne said? That she was unmarried at the moment and without a permanent home? All Daphne's fault, she thought sharply, as she handed over the jug of milk. Thoughts in my head, words in my mouth.

'I look forward to that,' Stephen said as he took the jug and headed for the door. 'Thanks for the drink, and this.'

He nodded at the jug, looked back at her, tripped and slopped milk over the pristine floor.

'Sorry!'

Cross with herself for being so easily charmed, now Mel couldn't wait to get him out of her way.

'It's OK. Just milk,' she said snappily and he grinned as he made his way down the stairs, glancing back over his shoulder again.

'And no use crying over the spilling of it, I'd say. Good-night now, Melanie. I'll be seeing you sometime.'

He disappeared. Mel returned to her chair by the window but something had gone from the room, from the flat. She spent the rest of the evening wondering about this unusual friend of Daphne's who obviously bumbled through the world, managing to charm everybody he met without actually saying anything very much. As to seeing him sometime, well, she decided her life was far too busy to entertain such a meeting.

*   *   *

The mobile phone rang just as she was leaving
the flat, taking a basket of picnic food to Becky
so that the final delivery to Julia Wells at the
rectory could be made. Mel put the box of
goodies on the hall table and spoke with a
touch of irritation.

'Mel Brooks here.'

'James Chandler,' she heard in a cool,
smooth voice that sounded pleasant despite all
she'd heard about its owner.

She'd been half expecting his call. Curiosity
grew and she spoke in a friendlier tone of
voice.

'I'm in a bit of a rush. May I ring you back?'

'Better than that, Mel, why don't we meet
for lunch?'

Mel? And they hadn't even met? She
frowned, thinking he sounded too sure of
himself, and of her.

'Can you manage that?' he asked.

Quickly she assessed the situation. Why
not? He probably wanted to talk about
Daphne and she must go along with that.
'All right. About half twelve? Where?'

'The little Italian place in Swallow Row here
in Newton. Do you know it?'

She'd been there once or twice with
Andrew. Push back the memories, she
decided.

'Yes,' she said. 'Thank you, James. I'll be there. Goodbye.'

She drove to Becky's house where they both packed all the food, plates and drinks into the small green van that was the business transportation. Then Becky went off to deliver the picnic goodies and Mel drove into town, wondering wryly what James Chandler would make of her working gear of linen trousers and pale blue silk shirt.

He was waiting at a table beneath an awning in the small, traffic-free precinct that surrounded the banks of the river flowing through the town. In an elegant dark suit, pristine cream shirt, trendy haircut, he was sophistication epitomised, vastly different from Stephen Summers!

James stood up, smiling, holding out his hand.

'Good of you to come. Do sit down. Now, what will you drink?'

Mel asked for a spritzer and then said, 'James,' but got no further.

His very pale eyes were intent on her face and his expression wasn't exactly businesslike. She did hope he wasn't going to get too friendly.

She sat back and said coolly, 'Why do you want to talk to me? I suppose it's about Daphne.'

She saw his smile vanish.

'Yes,' he said shortly. 'My aunt is a difficult,

old woman.'

Mel snapped.

'She's a good friend of mine, and I don't like to hear you speak about her in that way.'

At once the silky smile returned and he put his elbows on the table and regarded her across steepled fingers. His voice was seductive.

'And how lucky she is to have you as a friend, Mel. Yes, of course, I understand how you feel about her, and she is, after all, my aunt. Blood runs thicker than water, you know. Let's hope you and I can somehow persuade her to think a bit more constructively about Glebe Cottage!'

Mel thought, so this is what it's all about, the sale of the house—and the garden. Her heart sank, but for Daphne's sake she'd listen to James. Perhaps she could undermine his selfish plans in some way.

'I don't think Daphne realises that Glebe Cottage is likely to be sold, James,' she said coolly. 'She has plans to return there, when she's able.'

'Rubbish!' he said and she watched his colour flare. 'From what I hear, the old girl's too decrepit to go back again. Surely she's not too far gone to know that.'

Mel was now getting very cross. She sipped her drink and looked into his watchful eyes.

'She probably knows,' she told him sharply, 'but she's not admitting it. You see, no-one has told her directly that she won't go home. I think she should be left to make up her own mind about the future of Glebe Cottage.'

For a moment they stared at each other. Then James answered slowly.

'You realise I'm her next of kin, do you, and her solicitor? As such I have a duty towards her and her financial situation. She's probably very confused, uncertain about all the money matters. I can sort them out for her.'

Mel nodded thoughtfully. It all seemed horribly clear, and inevitable. But she wasn't going to bulldoze poor Daphne into something she wasn't ready to do just yet. James must be made to understand that.

'I think you should let things lie for a bit, James. It'll happen in the end, but what's the rush?'

'No rush,' he said, quickly, but Mel thought there was no conviction in the words.

When would they get to the point of this meeting, she wondered. Then she decided to play it her way.

'Shall we eat?' she asked lightly. 'I've got a busy afternoon.'

'Of course.'

He signalled the waiter and together they looked at the menu. Agreeing on their mutual choice of warm leaves and smoked salmon mayonnaise, Mel took the opportunity of waiting for the food to arrive to speak.

'I imagine you want me to do something,

James. What is it exactly?'

He stared across the table, the easy smile sliding into a tighter expression.

'You don't miss a trick, do you? But I like feisty women!'

Suddenly the seductive smile returned, but only for a moment.

'Well, this is it. Aunt Daphne's always been a bit of a mystery. You probably know that?'

Mel nodded. Where was this leading?

'So, if I can be of any assistance to her, I really need to have access to the cottage.'

'Why?'

Instantly, Mel was on the defensive. Then she remembered the notebook and pen left in Daphne's kitchen. If it wasn't James who had been there, who was it?

He sighed impatiently.

'Because I must look at her papers. You know, bank statements, investments, make sure she hasn't made another will somewhere, things like that. We all know how old ladies get up to funny tricks, don't we?'

'You may think so, James, but I'm very sure that your aunt hasn't been up to anything, except to suffer a heart attack. She's absolutely clear in her mind, always has been, and still is. And anyway, if you want the key to Glebe Cottage why can't you just ask her for it?'

'Because she won't give it to me. I know that, even without asking.'

His voice was abruptly heavy. Mel paused as

their meal arrived.

'Really? And why's that, then?' she asked when they were alone again.

James grinned rather unpleasantly over the table.

'Because I'm not exactly the black sheep of the family, but the nephew she never liked or spent time with. Dear old Aunt Daphne and I never got on, you see.'

Yes, she did see, rather too much for her liking. James must have done something very nasty to make Daphne practically disown him. And now he hoped she would get the key from Daphne and pass it over, so that he could ransack all her private papers, did he! No way! For a moment Mel wanted to throw her salmon mayonnaise straight at his handsome face.

Instead, she said carefully, 'So you'd like me to get the key on some pretext or other and then hand it over to you, is that it? Is that why you're treating me to this expensive meal today?'

His reaction was to drop knife and fork on his plate and stare at her, clearly surprised.

'Now, come on, Mel, you make it sound like a terrible old black and white movie where wicked nephew plans to plunder rich relative's home by stealth, or something!'

Mel smiled sweetly.

'And that's exactly what it sounds like, James. Well, I think you should do whatever you think you need to do, but without involving me. OK? And now let's talk about something else, shall we? This salmon really is delicious. I hope you're enjoying yours as much as I am.'

She met his eyes and was astonished to see honest admiration in them. He laughed, and said reluctantly, 'I suppose I deserved that! You really are a friend worth having! I hope Aunt Daphne realises your value.'

Mel smiled in return. Perhaps he hadn't meant to be quite so upfront and hasty as she'd thought. Perhaps he wasn't trying anything on, just a busy man grudgingly taking up long-neglected responsibilities. She thawed slightly.

'I certainly value her friendship and I believe the feeling is returned,' she said, 'and if you really think it would help Daphne if you took over all her responsibilities, well, I might just mention your name.'

'Watch out if you do!'

Then, for a second or two, he said no more. She glanced up, met his eyes, and saw a strange expression of triumph in them. But his next words were quiet and grateful.

'Thanks, Mel. I'd really be glad if you'd do that, and now, as you said, let's talk about something else. Tell me about this fantastic catering business you run. I've heard excellent reports of it.'

They said goodbye after coffee and Mel

drove back to the village, her head overflowing with echoes of what James had said about Daphne's papers, a possible second will, made without his knowledge, her finances. Of course, as her next of kin and solicitor, James certainly needed access to these important things, but for her to get the key from Daphne and then pass it on to him, knowing how Daphne felt about him? Mel squirmed as she parked outside Becky's house and wished she hadn't promised to put in a word for him. She couldn't help feeling that she'd let herself into something that eventually she would regret.

She and Becky drove to the picnic area by the river where Julia Wells and her family were gathering together their belongings ready to return home.

'A super meal. We've eaten every scrap!' Julia said effusively.

'Good,' Becky said, piling empty dishes into the van that she'd left parked beneath the oak trees. 'So recommend us, will you? Nothing like word of mouth, you know!'

'I certainly will,' Julia said. 'I hear you've got a new neighbour, by the way, Mel. You know how gossip gets around, like Becky said. Stephen Summers, isn't it?'

Mel turned from packing plates into baskets and stared at Julia. 'Yes, that's his name. Do you know him?'

'No!' Julia laughed. 'But I'm sure I've heard it somewhere. Now, let me see . . .'

Her voice rose abruptly as her eyes swivelled to look back at the children. 'Oh, Daniel, Sandy, stop doing that!'

Mel watched her fly off and part the two elder boys who were happily hitting each other with fallen branches. But what on earth did she know about Stephen Summers? Well, too late to bother now. The family car was being filled with chattering children and Julia quickly drove off.

Mel finished the packing up, shut the van door and went round to the driving seat as Becky switched on the ignition.

'Doing much this afternoon, Becky?'

'Clearing up, as usual.'

'Leave it,' Mel said firmly. 'I'll help when I bring Susi home. Look, why not come and help us in Daphne's garden, just for an hour? OK, OK!' she added as Becky put on an exaggerated expression of horror. 'You can sit on the bench and watch us work. Come on, Becky, do you good to get away from the kitchen on a hot day like this.'

Becky's plump, girlish face slid into pleasant anticipation.

"Lovely,' she said. 'Sure, I'll come. Just an hour, mind, and don't expect any floral conversation, will you? I may be cordon bleu trained but I'm definitely not literate in botany.'

Mel decided the garden already looked a little tamer today, but there was still much to do. She organised Becky on the bench in the shade, giving her the sun hat she usually wore, and settled Susi in a cool place, digging up a group of plants before they could seed themselves. Then, arming herself with a spade, she attacked a huge mountain of couch grass that was growing among a clump of lilies.

'How d'you know what you're doing?' Becky asked and Mel grinned.

'I don't. Just reading books and hoping for the best. But tell you what, I'm actually enjoying it. Andrew and I didn't.'

She stopped abruptly.

'I mean, I haven't had a garden since I was a child,' she continued shortly, 'and didn't ever think I'd have one again.'

'Ah,' Becky said soothingly, 'maybe it's time for a change. I recommend finding a new life.'

Mel glanced over her shoulder and said scathingly, 'Oh? Then why aren't you out there, looking for yours?'

'Just filling in time until the right man comes along.' Suddenly Becky's lazy voice awoke.

'Hey! And who might this be?'

Both Susi and Mel looked up.

'It's a man,' Susi said importantly and her mother grinned, sitting more sedately, running a hand through her untidy hair.

'I'll say it is!' Becky agreed.

Mel straightened up.

'It's Stephen,' she said coolly, 'my new

neighbour. He's a friend of Daphne's, and probably come to get something for her from the cottage.'

She bent again to the spade, refusing to make too much of Stephen's arrival, but she knew her face had flushed and was furious with the reaction. Becky was already mustering all her flirtatious powers.

'Hi!' she called as Stephen came to a sudden stop halfway up the path. 'Don't mind us! We're just the workforce. Can we help you in some way?'

By now Susi had sidled up to the bench. Mel, from the corner of her eyes, saw Stephen smile down at her as he replied pleasantly.

'What a wonderful place to work in. Any vacancies? I wouldn't mind signing on myself.'

Becky slid up the bench, pulling Susi with her, making extra space.

'Come and sit down first. You can share my sun hat if you like. I'm Becky and this is Susi.

'I suppose you know Mel—well, I mean, obviously, as she knows you.' Her tone was dry and Mel guessed this wasn't the last she'd heard about not introducing this very personable man to her friend straight away.

Stephen sat down on the end of the bench and said, 'Five minutes, that's all I can spare. I'm workforce, too, you see.'

'Really? What do you do?' Becky asked, blatantly curious.

But Stephen turned to Susi and changed the

subject.

'You must be the gardener's mate. Any tips for me?'

Susi considered, then bestowed one of her angelic smiles on him. 'I know about magic,' she said importantly.

'Ah, tell me.'

Mel, hating herself because she couldn't help watching and listening to this exchange, saw the skin crinkle around his eyes and guessed he was enjoying himself. Susi marched across to the herb bed and picked a sage bloom.

'The fairies ring these bells when they need help.'

She went to his side, thrusting the flower almost into his face.

'Can you hear them?'

Stephen took the flower, turning it in his big hands, almost tenderly, Mel thought, as if he were used to talking to children. His own family, perhaps? Suddenly she felt unbearably envious of Stephen's possible family. She braced herself, dug viciously at a root of grass and tried not to think.

'No, I can't hear anything, not yet. But perhaps if danger threatens . . .'

He was looking into Susi's delighted eyes, patiently waiting for her next revelation. It bounded out of her.

'And Miss Chandler said there's a dragon plant somewhere. What do you think it does?'

'Fight bad things?'

'Yes!' Susi crowed. 'Do you know which one it is?'

Stephen bent down so that he was on her level, looking at her very seriously.

'I don't, but tell you what, I'll find out. Then I can tell you and you can look for it here in the garden.'

'When? When will you do it?'

Susie was enchanted and hopped about, standing beside him. Becky interrupted.

'Susi, don't be a pest. I bet Stephen has other things to do than look for dragons.'

'You're right,' he said and stood up, smiled a last time at Susi, and said, 'I'll put the dragon plant on my list.'

Mel, understanding that he was keen to get back to his mysterious work, heard Becky quickly trying diversionary tactics, her voice heavily seductive.

'That's kind of you, Stephen. Don't mind if I call you that, do you? Mel didn't introduce us properly. Tell us all about yourself. I can't wait to hear.'

Mel, on her knees now, struggling with the last six inches of sinister white root, kept her face down, not wanting Becky to see her thoughts, but nevertheless listening avidly. Would he tell Becky more than he'd told her last night, which was precisely nothing? Now she realised he was doing the same with Becky.

'I'm a friend of Daphne Chandler's, and as I

heard so much about the famous paradise garden I thought I'd drop in and see it. I'm glad I did. It's a beautiful garden and a fantastic workforce.'

Mel heard the wry amusement but wouldn't allow herself to look up and see the accompanying smile.

'But now I guess I'd better get on with some real work.'

He nodded at Becky, then sauntered along the path until he stood beside Mel, on her knees.

'Daphne asked me for a few private things from her bedroom. I won't be long about it.'

Feeling his eyes on her back, Mel straightened up grudgingly.

'I don't know why you should bother to tell me,' she said tautly. 'If she's given you a key, then that's your affair, not mine. Go ahead.'

She received the full impact of his gaze, before he smiled casually.

'Right. Then I'll not bother you any more. Cheers,' he said and proceeded on his way up the path towards the front door.

She knew Becky and Susi were listening and watching. As soon as Stephen had disappeared into the cottage, Becky spoke crossly.

'What's got into you, Mel? Heat stroke or something? Such a charming chap, and all you can do is brush him off.'

Mel looked at her friend's bright, shrewd eyes and knew she could never deceive Becky.

They'd been close friends for too long for that, but now, for the first time, she needed to hide all she was feeling. Stephen's undoubted attraction, and, worse than that, Becky's easy, flirtatious manner which he had obviously found appealing, was making her into a different person, someone who needed privacy and safety; someone who was slowly and reluctantly realising that, after all, she longed for love in her life.

Susi returned to her digging, muttering about hoping he would hurry up and find out about the dragon plant, and Becky lay full length on the bench, eyes closed, clearly not inviting further conversation. When the cottage door banged shut and Stephen again walked down the path, Mel saw he was putting a notebook into his jacket pocket. So he had been here the other day. Her curiosity grew. What exactly was the little job Daphne had spoken of? Why should he keep coming to the cottage, and where was he going now?

'See you again soon, I'm sure,' he said as he smiled down at Becky, hardly glancing in Mel's direction.

'That'll be nice,' Becky told him, with an inviting smile of her own. 'Come and see my garden any time. Susi and I are always at home, alone.'

Mel was fuming. Really, Becky was preposterous! Of course she was only joking, as she always did, but what was Stephen's reaction to such brazen behaviour? She gave him a hard look, but he was again stooping down beside Susi, helping her blow the groundsel clocks away.

' 'Bye, Susi,' he said, standing up.

Mel saw how the child watched him walk away, go out of the gate, and disappear. She had the same look on her face that came when she talked about magic and Mel knew that all of them in the garden had fallen under Stephen Summers' mysterious spell.

Quickly, she downed tools, persuaded Becky and Susi it was teatime, and drove them home. She couldn't wait to get back to the quiet serenity of Dunmore House where she could jump back into being her right-minded self, Mel Brooks, independent career girl who had no need of men.

CHAPTER THREE

At the Grange next day Melanie learned that Daphne had taken a turn for worse, not another attack, but she was feeling very weak. Mel was asked not to stay too long.

Daphne was in bed, a small shape beneath the duvet. She opened her eyes when Mel came into the room and managed a smile and Mel recognised that even that was a challenge to her strength.

'I brought you a hazelnut meringue,' Mel said cheerily, putting a paper bag on the bed table. 'Left over from Julia Wells' picnic yesterday. I know you like them.'

'Thank you, my dear. When I feel a little better. Do sit down.'

Mel did as she was told and looked anxiously at the pale face which, in repose, seemed older than usual. She thought for a moment, wondering whether to leave James's request until a more suitable occasion, but Daphne surprised her by speaking quietly, pausing between sentences.

'I wanted to see you. I'm glad we're alone. Melanie . . .'

'Yes, Daphne?'

The business of talking was clearly difficult. Mel took one tiny, frail hand in hers and held it, wishing she could inject some energy into Daphne's weak body. And then, as if it had actually happened, Daphne looked at her very directly, and went on in a stronger voice.

'I've been thinking hard lately. I'm old and I'm unwell. I would like to return to my home, but I'm beginning to think it's highly unlikely, and there are things there that I'm worried about.'

'Anything I can do for you, Daphne, just ask.'

'In my bedroom, there is a certain photograph, a young man in uniform, and some papers, important papers. I would be happier if they were here with me. You see . . .'

Mel waited and after a short pause, Daphne sighed and continued.

'Well, never mind all that. It's just I want you to have the key to Glebe Cottage and go and find me the things I've mentioned. And, Melanie no-one else is to use that key, you understand?'

'Yes, of course, Daphne.'

Mel was confused. Did Daphne remember that she must have given a second key to Stephen Summers? Or had he somehow broken into the cottage? In which case, what was he up to? Her thoughts ran riot for a moment, but then she focused them on the immediate situation.

'Daphne, I have to ask you about your nephew, James. He is, after all, your next of kin, and as your solicitor, shouldn't he be the one to go into the cottage and find your papers?'

'I don't think so. I can just imagine him rummaging about in my bureau, in my bedroom.'

Mel tried again, although she was worried at the sudden patches of colour suddenly staining the old lady's cheeks.

'Actually, he's told me that he feels responsible and would like to do all he can to help you.'

Not exactly true, she thought wryly, but halfway there. She wished she hadn't agreed to put his case for him. Clearly Daphne had never trusted him, but it was too late for her to change now.

'James and I always disliked each other. And then there was the money.'

Daphne opened her eyes wide, stared at Mel and then added, 'But I won't go into that. Well, if James is really concerned, and I know he's very good with figures, the only thing he can do for me is to look at my investments and make sure that I have enough money to pay these nursing home fees. I don't wish to find myself bankrupt, do I? Yes, let's give him another chance.'

A smile softened the bony face.

'So yes, perhaps, after all, James may be given my financial papers, Melanie, but nothing else. You'll find them clearly marked in my bureau. And please make sure that he doesn't run off with any of my treasures! He always had light fingers!'

Mel saw with relief that Daphne's colour had become normal again, but clearly making her wishes known had been enough for her.

'I'll do exactly as you ask, Daphne,' Mel said and got up from the chair. 'Just tell me where the key is and then I'll leave you in peace. You need lots of rest, and I want you to have enough strength to enjoy your meringue at teatime!'

Daphne nodded.

'Look in my purse, in my handbag, and

guard it with your life, please, Melanie!'

The words were dramatic, but the smile was relaxed even amused, and Mel left the room with an easier mind.

Back in her car, she slipped the key into the zip-up compartment of her bag, and knew she'd be thinking about its safety every moment from now on. She drove through the village towards Glebe Cottage, looking at the garden as she went towards the entrance, thinking gladly that it really did seem a little more paradise-like, and then, unlocking the front door, let herself into the cottage.

Without Daphne, Glebe Cottage seemed sad and deserted. Mel wandered from room to room, noticing how quickly dust had formed on once-polished surfaces, how a musty smell replaced Daphne's favourite floral scents. It seemed that the little house had given up hope and was all too quickly allowing itself to slip into neglect. Climbing the stairs, Mel came to a decision. She must either find someone to come in and clean up the place, or do it herself. But how could she find the time?

Shaking her head, she went towards Daphne's bedroom and stood quite still in the doorway. Why be so negative? She was here for a purpose, so get on with it. The photograph of the young man in uniform stood in a big silver frame on the dressing table. With his thick, wavy fair hair, intelligent eyes and a warm, infectious smile, he stared back at her. Mel picked up the frame. Who was this man? Part of Daphne's mysterious past and plainly very important to her, but surely he must be dead by now? This was a photo of a soldier fighting in the Second World War. He must have been about twenty when the photo was taken, so did Daphne still carry a torch for him?

Mel shook her head, slipped the photo into her shoulder bag and then went across to the window, beside which stood the oak bureau where Daphne kept all her private papers. There was a key in the lock and for a moment she felt reluctant to intrude on a life that must hold so many secrets. The bureau opened smoothly and in the small, narrow drawers inside Mel saw clearly-labelled envelopes. One was Daphne's will and another was marked INVESTMENTS. The last one bulged with what she supposed were letters, a photo or two, some postcards, and something large and bulky which took up most of the envelope.

Again, Mel packed the envelopes Daphne had asked for into her bag, relocked the bureau, and then, on an impulse, pocketed the key. Why, she wasn't sure, but two things niggled at the back of her mind. James wanted access to the cottage and Stephen already had it. So she'd keep the bureau key herself, just in case.

She left hurriedly, relieved to cast off the gloom of the empty house. Outside, her mood lightened as she went towards the gate, quickly assessing all the work done so far. Yes, there was still a lot to be done, but she and Susi would be here again tomorrow. They wouldn't give up.

At home, grabbing a quick sandwich, Mel talked to Becky on her mobile.

'I've arranged to go down and see a client who phoned last night, who wants to discuss our catering for a garden party in September, somewhere out on the moor, so I might be a bit late to collect Susi.'

'That's OK,' Becky said. 'I've done all the cooking ready for tomorrow's contract so I'll fetch her myself. Hey, Mel, nearly forgot to tell you. That dishy Stephen's come up with a print-out of what he called Susi's dragon plant! Great, isn't it? I think he's a really nice guy. Glad you're not likely to be interested. I quite fancy him myself!'

Becky's laugh was jokey, but Mel sensed an undercurrent of more serious intent. She tried to join in with Becky's humour but found it hard to keep so lighthearted when her mind was busy running round in circles.

'Susi will be pleased,' she managed, 'Yes, very good of him. A printout? I didn't realise he brought a computer with him when he moved in.'

'I don't think we know nearly enough about him,' Becky suggested, still laughing. 'Why not give the guy a chance to tell us? Go down and offer him one of our Devon farm suppers. He'd probably jump at the chance of a decent meal. And then you can invite me, too, and we'll find out all about him. Yes?'

'No,' Mel said firmly. 'Go and get on with your jam making or whatever's next on the list and stop bothering me. I'll see you tomorrow.'

'OK, but keep your hair on, girl. Seems to me you're getting in a hassle over nothing.'

And with that the line went dead.

Mel ate her sandwich absentmindedly and then set out to see the next potential client. When she came back, she told herself, she must visit Daphne and then phone James.

*   *   *

'Miss Chandler is asleep and we don't really want to wake her as she had a bad night,' the nurse said when Mel arrived at the nursing home. 'Can I take a message?'

Uncertainly Mel asked, 'Do you think she'll be well enough for visitors tomorrow?'

'Probably. Ring in the morning and see what sort of night she's had. Who shall I tell her called?'

'Say it's Melanie, and please tell her I've got all the things she asked me to fetch from her home. I'll look after them until I see her. Give her my love, won't you?'

Mel returned to her car, anxiety growing. It seemed unthinkable that Daphne could be fading away. Her energy had always been one of the amazing things about her. And if Daphne should die without reconciling her unhappy relationship with James, what would happen? Would Glebe Cottage be sold? And what would happen to her beloved garden?

Mel drove home feeling badly in need of support from someone. She rang Becky but there was no answer, and she guessed Becky and Susi were having a trip out somewhere. After a long, thoughtful pause, she phoned James. When he answered, she tried not to keep her voice businesslike.

'Hi, James, it's Mel. About your aunt's belongings . . .'

But at once she could hear him smiling down the line as he said, 'Mel! Great to hear you. Have any luck with the old girl, did you?'

'Your aunt wasn't well enough to see me when I called today. So I couldn't talk to her. In the meantime . . .'

He interrupted quickly.

'Get the papers, did you? That's the important thing.' Mel couldn't help exploding.

'James, your poor aunt is old, and extremely ill. Haven't you any feelings for her at all?'

Silence followed for a second or two and she could imagine him wondering how to appease her, how to get the conversation back on the footing that he so badly wanted. Then he spoke in a quieter tone.

'Of course I have, but I'm a business man,

51

Mel, and my life is made up of solving people's problems for them. Surely you can see that I'm simply concerned that Aunt Daphne will pop off before I can sort out hers?'

Surprised at his sudden apparent sincerity, Mel felt a twinge of guilt for suspecting his ulterior motives.

'Of course,' she said quickly. 'I'm sorry. Actually, James, I've got her portfolio of investments and she's agreed to let you deal with them.'

'Great! Why don't I drop round and collect them? We could have a bite somewhere nearby. There's a very good restaurant out towards the moor, highly recommended.

Instinctively, Mel said, 'No, sorry, can't manage it. I—er—have a date tonight anyway.'

She crossed the fingers of her free hand and quickly continued.

'I'll bring the papers into town tomorrow and leave them at your office. Thanks for the invitation, James, but I must go now, cheers.'

She rang off in a hurry and stared at the phone, half afraid that he'd ring back. He didn't, and she was left sitting alone, wondering at the ease with which she'd made up an excuse not to see him when she knew, deep inside, that all she wanted this evening was a friend, someone to pass the time with, someone to talk to. No longer was it enough to be independent, living alone, forging a career.

It didn't take her long to face the need that

filled her. She had to admit to herself that she wanted to talk to Stephen Summers and once the truth was out she quickly found an excuse for calling on him. Of course! Susi's dragon plant. Without even thinking of changing her working gear for something smarter, Mel went downstairs. If she didn't do it at once, she knew she'd start regretting the impulse and spend the rest of the long evening alone.

But, as she rang the bell of the downstairs flat, her courage almost failed. What on earth would he think of her, calling on the flimsiest of pretexts? Surely she could have come up with something a bit more realistic than the plant! She almost fled at the last moment, but then the door opened and Stephen stood there, looking at her with those amazing sea-green eyes that saw everything and understood.

'Hi!' she said breathlessly. 'I've just come to—er—to thank you for finding out about Susi's dragon plant. I know she must be thrilled.'

Then she ran out of words. He knew, he understood, and she felt like a small child caught in the most obvious of crimes. Strangely, he seemed glad to see her.

'Come in, Mel. Good to see you. I owe you a drink. What'll you have?'

She entered the flat, acutely aware of the difference in the owner's choice of furniture and décor in comparison with her own self-furnished lovely home upstairs. Stephen followed her into the living-room, removing a pile of books from the comfiest-looking armchair, smiling as she sat down.

'Décor's not exactly my cup of tea, either,' he said wryly, and she guessed that her expression had said all she was thinking. 'But it's adequate for the time I have to be here. Now, a drink?'

Slowly her nerves were subsiding. She felt quite happy sitting there, with him towering above her, his smile warm and welcoming. Yes, she'd been right to come, but just a neighbourly call, nothing more.

'White wine would be great, thanks.'

He went into the kitchen and she took the opportunity to look around her. It was quite a large room, identical in size to her own living-room above, but cluttered with heavy, mahogany furniture, and crowded with papers, books, files, maps. They were heaped on the table in front of the window, almost hiding a computer and a telephone. Even the floor had piles of open books scattered at the base of the table. Clearly, Stephen was a busy man, but what sort of work was he engaged in? And, more importantly, what was he doing for Daphne? Dare she ask him?

She smiled as he came in again with glasses in his hand and said lightly, 'Seems I've disturbed you in the middle of things.'

She nodded at the table and then wondered

at her nosiness.

'I'm an untidy chap. Living alone is an excuse for never putting things in their proper places, but I'm sure you don't find the same.'

He sat down opposite her, nursing his glass of whisky and waiting for her to drink her wine. She took a sip, amused now at his own brand of nosiness. They seemed to be playing the same game.

'You're right. A place for everything and everything in its place is my motto. I drive Becky wild with my tidiness, and talking of Becky, it really was good of you to research Susi's magic plant.'

'Research is the name of my particular game,' he said, obviously amused, and Mel wondered if he'd read her thoughts on the subject of playing games. 'As you can see, I'm In the thick of things at the moment and so all my references have to stay where I can easily find them. It's a muddle. Is your wine OK?'

Mel took another, longer sip. It was certainly OK and so was she now, relaxed, and intrigued by all that Stephen was—and wasn't—revealing.

'It's great,' she replied, then she took a deep breath and dared to ask, 'So what exactly are you researching?'

His expression was suddenly impersonal and she realised he was a man who didn't welcome questions. Quickly she changed tack, smiling.

'Or is it a secret? Military intelligence

perhaps? That sort of stuff?' she added clumsily.

'Yes, it's secret work.' He was smiling again. 'But compelling. I enjoy what I do. As I imagine you do, too, Mel, but surely, all that cooking, 'specially on hot days like this, doesn't it get to you sometimes? Don't you ever long for an easy meal away from the oven, prepared by someone else?'

She laughed. Again, he'd changed the subject. How intriguing this was.

She said, without really thinking where the words might lead, 'I certainly do. I love cooking, but, as you say, a meal out is a huge treat.'

Stephen nodded and she saw his eyes light up mischievously.

'Well, then, you won't say no when I invite you to come out this evening and have a meal, will you?'

Mel's mouth dropped. She hesitated briefly, remembering James's invitation and her quick refusal. And then she surprised herself by accepting!

'Right. So drink up and we'll make a move. I know just the place.'

'I'll go upstairs and change into something a bit more presentable.'

'No, you won't. You look great.'

He lifted his glass to her and something unfamiliar sparked in Mel's mind. How long was it since she had allowed a man to take charge of her life, since a man had looked at her as Stephen was? Several years, it was, and, stranger than anything else, she didn't really mind. She had an intuitive feeling that he wouldn't take advantage of her, wouldn't make her feel helpless and subservient—but she still wished she could go and put on a more flattering dress!

'Finished? Then let's go.'

He was on his feet in one swift movement, leaving both empty glasses where they stood on the small table between the chairs.

She smiled as she followed him through the hall and out of the flat. Mel felt her enjoyment mounting. Stephen drove carefully out of the village, into the sleepy countryside. He turned left into a lane when she had expected him to drive straight along the main road towards Torquay and its selection of glitzy restaurants. He smiled each time he glanced at her. They didn't speak, but an atmosphere of relaxed companionship seemed to fill the car.

Eventually, he stopped in a small village halfway to the moor and Mel looked around her with surprise. Surely, no trendy eating places here? Stephen must have read her thoughts, for he turned to her.

'Fish and chips, I thought. OK with you? And I've got a favourite place for eating them. Cod or plaice, Mel?' he asked.

Stifling her amusement, she said, 'Oh, plaice, I think, please, Stephen,' and watched him walk down the pavement towards the nearby shop!

A large shabbily-dressed man with a charismatic, rather secretive air about him, he was almost irresistible to any woman, Mel thought wryly and then frowned. What about *Who Needs Men? Not Me!* One thing she knew for sure, this unexpected, outdoor feast definitely put paid to Becky's jazzy idea of inviting him to a home-cooked supper. Obviously, Stephen Summers was no ordinary man, and as such his rather unconventional ideas must be respected.

When he returned, he stowed the fragrant parcels of food on the back seat and drove off again.

'I expect you know Luckford Bridge, but I only found it the other day,' he said as he turned into yet another lane where the trees almost met over the car. 'Wonderful place, water, wild life, and nobody else there.'

Turning briefly, he smiled into her wide eyes and she realised he was teasing again, testing her, discovering if her reactions were what he was expecting. She mustn't let him down.

'I haven't been to Luckford since I was a child. It was a magic place.'

His smile was approving and Mel felt their rapport growing.

'Well, here we are.'

He parked the car beneath tall, thickly-canopied trees. The heat of the day had lessened to a welcome cool breath of fresh moorland air, and the little stream beside them gurgled as it flowed on its way. For a moment, Mel stood and looked at the bubbling water, and thought about her happy childhood. She wished suddenly that Susi were here, to make dams, as she had once done, to catch elusive tiny sticklebacks, and to enjoy nature's simply beauty. Suddenly a streak of vivid peacock blue-green flew down the stream and she caught her breath.

'A kingfisher! Stephen, did you see it?'

He was beside her, smiling gravely, almost, she thought, as if he'd engineered the bird's flight especially for her benefit.

'Saw it when I was here before. Definitely a magic place. Now, where do you want to sit and have your supper?'

They shared a large rock on the bank of the stream. Mel thought that fish and chips had never tasted so good.

She ate in silence, until Stephen, licking his fingers as he finished eating, said, 'Good of you to call in and thank me for finding Susi's dragon plant. I was hoping to see you sometime.'

She couldn't think what to say, but he went on.

'Susi's a lovely kid, and they're such fun at that age. I always wanted a daughter.'

His voice was quiet and as Mel glanced at

him, she saw him staring at the flowing waters as if seeing someone there. Abruptly she felt the increasing coolness of the evening air. Daphne had said he was unmarried at the moment but that meant little these days. So why should she have imagined he was free? Clearly he wasn't.

'Still time, isn't there?' she said and then wished she hadn't.

What business was it of hers? He must think her incredibly nosey, asking such personal questions. But, to her surprise, he turned and looked at her very directly.

'I should like to think there is, but my wife died eighteen months ago and I live alone.'

He smiled, without much amusement, watched her reaction of obvious sympathy, and then reached out, putting his hand on hers.

'It's all right. No need to look like that. You're a warm, caring girl. I just wanted you to know.'

Mel nodded. Again, she could find no words. His hand warm and strong over hers, Stephen went on.

'I sold our family home and that's why I'm renting the flat at Dunmore House. I'm engaged on academic research, so I spend a lot of time in Cambridge. Don't have a permanent home any more.'

He paused, then removed his hand.

'I thought you should know the situation. You and Becky and young Susi have been very welcoming and friendly, but I shall be on my way again shortly. My little job for Daphne Chandler is nearly completed, you see.'

He grinned at her, a wry, deprecating, rather unhappy smile, she thought.

'I don't live anywhere very long. Perhaps it's time I settled down. I'm not sure. One of these days, maybe.'

Mel felt the foolish dream she'd been building collapse inside her. She had known, right at the moment of first seeing Stephen, that she was treading on quicksand. She didn't want another failed relationship, and, clearly, he didn't even want friends. She took in a huge breath and tried to be positive. Well, things hadn't gone too far, just a fish-and-chip supper by a singing stream on a magical July evening. Easy to forget. Easy to get on with life and let Stephen go on his own way.

Easy? For an agonised moment she faced the truth. Almost impossible, feeling as she did. But she would do it. Getting to her feet, she crumpled up the fishy newspapers and walked back towards the car.

'Midges about,' she said over her shoulder. 'Time to go, isn't it?'

'If you say so,' Stephen said and for a moment she turned and looked at him, seeing the same brief flash of disappointment on his face that she knew was showing on her own.

But it only lasted a second.

'Right,' he said briskly. 'Let's be on our

way.'

CHAPTER FOUR

Mel and Stephen had parted in a friendly, if final, way when they returned to Dunmore House.

'Thanks for coming out, Mel. I enjoyed your company,' he had said as he watched her climb the stairs before going into his own flat and she had smiled over her shoulder, trying hard to ignore the unwanted disappointment she felt.

'Good-night, Stephen.'

And goodbye . . .

She closed the door and resolutely refused to allow herself to think of anything except what the next day held. Sharing his confidence had been a one-off thing that he probably regretted even now. Without doubt, once away from Dunmore House, Stephen wouldn't bother to think of her again. Just as she wouldn't think of him. There was a lot of work building up, new clients always phoning and asking for interviews and quotes as well as all the usual everyday business chores. Also, she'd promised Daphne to try and clean Glebe Cottage, and the garden was still waiting.

First things first, Mel thought with a surge of new energy as she rang the nursing home to enquire about Daphne. There was a guarded response.

'She had a better night, but still feels weak. If you're coming to visit don't stay long, will you?'

Mel sent her love and said she'd be along sometime later. Then she drove into Newton with Daphne's portfolio of investments and handed them to the receptionist in James's office. No way did she want to see him. James Chandler was a volatile character, and although he was certainly a charmer, she was unsure about his motives. Better to keep him at a distance until he revealed himself more clearly.

She shopped at the supermarket on the way home, dropping off the groceries at Becky's house and fielding unwanted questions.

'Any chance of seeing Stephen if I bring Susi along this afternoon after school? She's keen to thank him for the dragon plant stuff, and I could give you a hand with the garden. Yes?'

'Come if you have time, but don't bank on seeing him. He's off soon. Not staying much longer,' Mel said carefully.

Becky stared.

'How do you know?'

'He told me.'

'When? You never said you'd got together.'

'And what's that supposed to mean?' Mel snapped. 'We're neighbours, that's all. He probably told me when we met at our mutual front door.'

'Hey, keep your hair on!'

Becky made two mugs of coffee and pushed one over the kitchen table.

'You're in a state, aren't you?'

'No,' Mel said very firmly. 'I'm just extremely busy, and I haven't got time for anything except figuring out how I'm going to clean Daphne's cottage as well as restoring her wretched garden. And it'd be far more helpful if you came up with a few ideas about that instead of imagining stupid things about Stephen and me.'

Becky looked across the table, nodded, and said quietly, 'Sorry, Mel. I know I'm the all-time busybody. Forget it. OK, then, you need a cleaning lady. I'll ring Alice Smith. Remember, she used to help out when Daphne expected visitors.'

Mel sighed, ashamed of her ill temper. Becky was a good friend and she was grateful for any help she could get.

'Right,' she said. 'I don't suppose Daphne would mind Alice going into the cottage. Give me her number, Becky. I'll ring her myself.'

Alice Smith said of course she'd be pleased to come and help out, would tomorrow morning, ten till twelve, do? And would Mel please give Miss Chandler her best wishes.

Mel tidied up all the waiting jobs on her desk, had a quick lunch and then drove to Glebe Cottage. Today it seemed natural to get cracking in the garden and, yes, things were improving. It was easy to see the big clumps of golden achillea now that the couch grass growing everywhere had been dug out. The huge buddleia bush by the wall was in full flower, its fragrance filling the garden, and the long purple tassels were decorated with nectar-sipping peacock's eye butterflies. Mel grinned, guessing that Susi would definitely connect her magic with these beautiful creatures.

She worked steadily, conscious of the sun on her back and bare arms, of the earth beneath her fingernails and, for the first time, understood a little of Daphne's passion for gardening. It was quiet out here, just birdsong and the lazy hum of bees. And there was a wonderful sense of serenity. Nothing seemed to matter except the next job, a forkful of earth or another pile of weeds to throw in the barrow.

She almost wished she had a garden at Dunmore House, and then Becky and Susi arrived and the peace was shattered.

'It's called taggaron—no, I mean tarragon,' Susi shouted from the gate, charging up the path and thrusting a piece of printed paper under Mel's nose. 'He gave me this, Stephen did, and it's a herb. I can't remember the real name. It's difficult to say, but it means a little dragon. I'll find it and pick a bit for Miss Chandler.'

Mel stood up and looked at Becky.

'Daphne's going downhill, I'm afraid,' she said soberly, 'and I want her to know that her garden's looking better. Lend a hand, Becky, will you? Between us we could make a real difference.'

Becky sighed.

'There goes my hope of a snooze in the sun,' she said then she grinned. 'Of course I'll help. So what do I do?'

They worked until Susi got tired and moaned that she needed a drink. Mel looked at Becky.

'I think we all do. Do you suppose Daphne would mind if I went into the kitchen and put on the kettle?'

Becky wiped the sweat off her brow and stood up very carefully, rubbing her back.

'This sort of stuff really gets the old muscles aching. Yes, what a super idea. A cup of tea would just about save my life. Of course Daphne wouldn't mind.'

With the tools put away in the shed and Susi's bunch of tarragon in her hand, they all went into the kitchen. It was cool in there and very soon Mel had found a teapot and a caddy of tea.

'Here, love, have your orange juice.'

Becky took the carton from her basket, poured a glassful for Susi and then measured out the tea.

'No teabags for Daphne,' she said

respectfully, reaching for the boiling kettle. 'Got the mugs, Mel? A pity I didn't think to bring some scones.'

But Mel wasn't listening. Was that a noise outside? Going to the open door she saw James Chandler walking towards her. He smiled brightly.

'Hi, Mel! Knew you'd be working on the old girl's garden. Just dropped by to thank you for getting the portfolio of her investments for me. I say!'

He looked over her shoulder, and beamed even more widely. 'Just in time for tea, am I? Great! Couldn't have timed it better, could I?'

'No, you couldn't,' Mel said coolly. 'Becky, this is James Chandler. Can that pot squeeze an extra cup, do you think?'

Becky looked at James with an aware gaze.

'Yes,' she said casually, 'I think I can manage one more. Sugar? Oh, but you're sweet enough, aren't you, James?'

Mel hid a smile at Becky's obvious distaste for the intruder. But why exactly was he here? Mel's thoughts began racing. Usually, with James, there was a reason for everything. Yes, he'd guessed she'd be here, with the key. Her mind cleared. It was so obvious. He needed to get into the cottage. She must be wary.

They drank their tea amid easy chatter. Susi's plant was examined and smelled with James showing no interest in the fact that it was a little dragon. Then Becky washed up

Susi's glass and the empty mugs and said it was time they went home.

'Things to do,' she said, winking at Mel and shepherding Susi out of the door.

'But I want to take the dragon plant to Miss Chandler,' Susi began.

'Tomorrow. She's not well enough for noisy, little visitors like you today,' Becky told her. 'Be in touch, will you?' she called to Mel as she followed Susi out. 'And don't forget that Alice will be here tomorrow morning.'

Over her shoulder she gave Mel a last, meaningful look.

'She hasn't got a key. Remember, you're the only one who has.'

Mel nodded.

'I'll be here. Cheers, Becky. 'Bye, Susi.'

She turned to James, standing watching.

'So, what do you want, James?'

His eyebrows rose.

'Hey, that's a rotten thing to suppose, that I only dropped in because I want something. Can't a guy visit a girl without becoming a suspect?'

His smile was impressive, but Mel saw beneath it. She went to the sink and washed her hands.

'I'm leaving, too. Time to get back and get on with my work.'

'Before you go, Mel.'

He came towards her, and as she turned she couldn't help thinking how calculating his

68

expression was.

'A favour, please.'

But his smile was warm and unexpectedly she found herself melting beneath it. She feared there was a sort of intimacy building between them and stepped back hastily.

'Depends what it is, James.'

'Nothing difficult. Am I allowed just a few moments in the garden while you're packing things away? Honestly, I won't steal any seeds, or cuttings.'

He was grinning and at once she felt foolish for suspecting him.

'Well, as long as you leave the statue in the pond, and don't ransack the garden shed, I suppose it's OK to let you loose.'

They both laughed.

'Right, I give you my promise, Mel.'

He ran a finger down her cheek before turning and going out into the garden and she didn't flinch.

Well, it was nice to be admired, Mel told herself. It was something she'd missed since Andrew left, if the truth were told, and no harm in letting James loose outside. As for his reason for being in the garden, well, he couldn't do any damage out there, could he? She cleared away the mugs, looked in the drawing-room to see that the curtains were drawn against prying eyes, and then went upstairs to Daphne's bedroom.

Standing in the doorway, she started

planning how to attack the increasing dirt and cobwebs. Perhaps tomorrow morning, when Alice was here, she would help by cleaning the windows, and then dust the ornaments and photographs standing on the mantelpiece and dressing table in the bedrooms. Did the old vacuum cleaner work? Well, she could always bring her own. It would be lovely to return Daphne's home to its previous pristine cleanliness. And one day she must go through the wardrobe, sorting out Daphne's clothes, take a few to the nursing home, perhaps.

James called from the garden.

'Mel? I daren't come in!'

His voice was jokey and she went downstairs, to find him standing in the kitchen doorway.

'Found what I was looking for. Remembered it from the old days when I used to visit Aunt Daphne. It's a four-leafed clover.'

He held out a small leaf and she raised an eyebrow. She hadn't thought that he was interested in anything but money.

'Lucky,' she said, and smiled.

'Just what I need.'

They looked at each other for a moment.

'Thought it might just turn my luck around with you, Mel,' he said and his voice softened as he came closer. 'You've got me hooked, did you know that? Any chance of wining and dining you one evening? No?' he added as she automatically shook her head. 'Well, put me on your list, will you? I'll wait.'

'Perhaps, but not yet.'

'OK, OK. I'll keep trying. You're a real cool chick, Mel.'

Again he stroked her cheek, grinning seductively.

'Cheers for now, then. See you soon, if my luck turns.'

He disappeared and she heard his car start up. She stayed in the doorway, thinking strange thoughts. Was James really such a baddie as Daphne had insisted he was? Even Becky, who considered every unattached man with interest, thought him a creep. But perhaps he'd changed. After all, he was no longer a rebellious adolescent but a mature man, with a charming manner, who admired her.

It was only as she left, turning to lock the front door after her, that she realised James's small favour of being let loose in the garden for five minutes had been a ploy to enable him to steal the key to Glebe Cottage from where she'd left it in the lock!

Glowering with rage and feeling a fool, she grabbed her mobile and punched in his number. No reply. Another call to his office brought a taped message. Mel slammed the phone into her bag and stormed out of the garden, knowing Daphne's home was being left open to the world. Her feeling of guilt was overpowering, even stronger than her fury with

James.

Driving home, she knew she must sort out her priorities. Did she go ahead with her promised visit to Daphne, or back to Dunmore House hoping that Stephen was there? She knew he had the second key to the cottage. He must hand it over so that she could go back and lock the door and then let Alice in tomorrow morning. Later, she would ring the Grange and leave a message for Daphne. Her mind a whirlwind of plans, she went home.

When she finally confronted Stephen, his response was as she had expected.

'My key? What's happened to yours?' he said, which didn't exactly help.

She had hoped to avoid having to explain what a fool she'd been to trust James, but clearly Stephen required a good reason for handing over his key, and she couldn't blame him. Looking down at her feet, she said, far more calmly than she felt, that James walked off with it.

She felt the sea-green gaze without meeting it. Slowly she looked up again. He was frowning and she hoped that his expression didn't reflect his thoughts of her.

'I see,' was all he said, but that was enough. 'Have you contacted him?'

'No. He's playing safe, not answering calls.'

'Naturally.'

A quizzical smile lifted Stephen's face.

'Right, here's my key. You're going there

72

again this evening?'

'Of course. I left it unlocked.'

They looked at each other for a moment and then Stephen said, 'Let me deal with Chandler. He doesn't know me so with any luck he'll answer my call. Come in for a moment.'

In the crowded living-room he gestured her to the armchair she'd sat in before and then, standing by the computer and riffling through some papers, picked up his mobile and punched in a number from the piece of notepad he'd found.

That's funny, Mel thought, how does he know James's number? And why was it on that bit of paper? One question followed another. What exactly is Stephen doing for Daphne? I wish I knew, and then she heard him speaking.

'James Chandler, please,' he said, and she winced at the coldness of his tone. 'My name is Stephen Summers. I'm calling about Miss Daphne Chandler, his aunt. He's busy? That's OK, I'll wait till he's free. I'll hang on.'

Mel imagined James's cautionary orders to his staff not to take any calls when he'd returned to the office, hers in particular, but she guessed that Stephen's unknown name and authoritative manner would bring results. She was right.

A minute later Stephen said, 'James Chandler? Stephen Summers here. Your aunt has commissioned me to act for her on a certain matter. I understand you're her solicitor, so I need to meet you for a discussion.'

In the background, James's voice said something, but Stephen quickly cut in.

'It's urgent. I shall be out of the area after tomorrow, so I'd be glad if you could manage either morning or afternoon.' He waited briefly, and then said, 'Let's say two thirty at Glebe Cottage. I'll see you then.'

Putting down the mobile he smiled across at Mel, and then came to stand by her chair. She'd been holding her breath in anticipation and now dared to smile back at him.

'That's fixed it,' he told her, and she guessed that the little exchange had amused him.

Stephen, she thought wryly, was an adversary whom James might well respect.

'Chandler will come like a lamb, because he's got to find out what I'm doing at the cottage.'

Suddenly Stephen took Mel's hands and pulled her carefully to her feet.

'Don't look like that,' he said, his voice altering, his eyes watching her with the gentle understanding that she'd first realised was his strong point. 'It'll all work out. I'll get the key back for you, Mel.'

Standing close to him, she was overcome with a longing so intense that she could hardly stop herself from pulling him even closer. Desperately she wanted to feel his arms around her. For a moment they stayed like that, and she thought wildly, go on, kiss me, please. But he didn't and she watched his expression grow tight and disturbed. He dropped her hands, stepped away.

'I'll get us a drink,' he said rapidly. 'You look upset. Hang on.'

He went towards the kitchen and she stood quite still, all her longing demolished by that sudden rejection. Thoughts circled her head dizzily. First there was James and his beastly trickery, and now Stephen, who clearly couldn't care less about her. She moved towards the table, where the computer screen flickered. Think about something else, she ordered herself. This was ridiculous. She must forget the attraction Stephen radiated. Not knowing what she was looking at, her gaze slid across the papers littering the table and suddenly her mind sprang to life again as she saw a familiar name.

CHANDLER was the heading on a piece of old, dog-eared paper that looked as if it had been folded, crumpled and forgotten. But it was here, on Stephen's worktop, and must be something to do with the little job Daphne had commissioned. Mel concentrated and saw that the paper was a handwritten family tree.

She read how Joseph Chandler, born 1865, married Margaret Barrett, and died in 1925, leaving two children called Edward and Daphne. Mel read on, spellbound, not caring that Stephen might object to her curiosity. Edward married and had a grandson called James. Daphne was unmarried, but something was scribbled in pencil under her name and Mel was just about to decipher it when Stephen came back with the drinks. But she had seen the letter **R** and a clear **A** at the end followed by another scribble.

She turned quickly, saw his eyes go to the paper behind her, and said off the top of her head, 'Sorry, I couldn't help seeing the name, Chandler. It's a family tree, isn't it?'

'Yes,' he said, taking the wine glasses to the two chairs by the window and waiting for her to follow him. 'Not very old, but interesting. Now, tell me what you're planning to do after you've been to the cottage to lock up. Got anything in mind?'

She took the glass from him and drank. It was cool, refreshing, and energising.

'I must come back here and answer my mail.'

'No time for fish and chips? Or perhaps you might even consider a proper meal? I understand Newton offers a selection of cuisines.'

So he wasn't going to tell her about the family tree. Did he think she wasn't to be trusted? Or perhaps he believed she was seeing too much of James. But she felt rejected all over again. First the near-embrace, and now the keep-off warning about the family

76

tree. She sat back in her chair, regarding him with the same awareness that he was focusing on her.

'Sorry,' she said lightly and with increasing self-control, 'but I really can't accept either invitation. Perhaps another time,' and then she realised she was treating him in the same distant way as she had treated James, as Becky would say, giving him the brush-off.

Before she could change her mind, he smiled and she thought resentfully, he really doesn't care.

'Drink up,' he said. 'Looks as if I'll have to invest in a freezer full of food, doesn't it? Might even have to learn to cook in the end.' But the accompanying quick flash of vivid smile failed to entertain her.

They drove in Stephen's car to Glebe Cottage, locked the door and then returned to Dunmore House. With the key safely in her bag, Mel thanked him for being so helpful, as she got out of the car and then tried not to look at him, as they walked towards the front door.

She turned as he opened it, thought the expression on his face was as grim as she felt her own to be.

'Good-night,' she said rapidly and went straight up the stairs.

Stephen made no reply, but she felt him watching her until she went into her own flat and closed the door. It was some time before she could get her mind to the work she wanted to do and even then, the question of Stephen having Daphne's family tree still lurked in the background. She railed at herself for not being honest enough to ask him what he was doing with it, and what those illegible words beneath Daphne's name meant, but she'd been too caught up in her feelings to do that.

It had been impossible to stop herself reliving the moment when Stephen had nearly kissed her, and then, for some reason, decided not to. Whose fault had that been? Hers, for showing how she felt too early in their relationship, or his because he didn't return her feelings?

The evening seemed longer and lonelier than usual and she wondered if Stephen was feeling the same way. Well, she thought brusquely, if he did, it was entirely his own fault.

In the morning, she hurried through the necessary chores before driving to Glebe Cottage and meeting Alice on the doorstep.

'Thought I'd tackle the upstairs while you do the kitchen and living-room, Alice,' she said, letting them in and finding cleaning equipment.

'My goodness,' Alice exclaimed, 'this old vacuum cleaner's been around for a long time, but there, Miss Chandler said it worked all right. I'll just give it a clean before I use it.'

It sounded fine, Mel thought, as she went

upstairs into Daphne's bedroom and looked around, uncertain where to start. She'd tackle the cobwebs first. Then take down the curtains and shake them, and windows next.

She worked until eleven thirty, and then called down to Alice to put on the kettle. Sitting around the kitchen table drinking coffee, she listened to Alice telling her about Daphne's love of children.

'I used to bring my little grandson sometimes,' Alice said, eyes alight with memories. 'Miss Chandler let him play in the garden, and often she'd be out there with him, telling him all about the flowers.'

Mel remembered Daphne talking to Susi in the same way.

'Such a shame she never married. What a marvellous grandma she'd have made,' Mel said.

Alice nodded her head.

'Well, I'd better get on. Two hours, you said, and it's nearly that now. Still, we've made a start. Want me to come again next week, Mel?'

'Between us we'll get the old place cleaned up, Alice. Yes, next Tuesday, please.'

She went upstairs again, concentrating this time on the dusty chest of drawers against the wall beside the window. There was something lodging behind the chest. She could see its outline, stuffed against the wall. Squinting down at it, she pulled the chest an inch or two into the room. At once the thing fell to the ground. She kneeled down, feeling beneath the floor of the chest. Got it!

It was a photo, large and dusty, a picture of a young woman holding a baby, looking straight into the camera. It was a photo taken in the past. The girl's clothes looked like the 1970s, she thought. Fascinated, she turned it over, saw some writing, faded and almost indecipherable but her heart leaped. The R and the A on Daphne's family tree now made sense—Rosa. The same letters here on the photo jigsawed into a believable fact. Very carefully, she dusted off the photograph, laid it on the bed and then pushed the chest back to its original place.

Rosa—she stared into the girl's face but learned nothing. There was no smile, no resemblances she could build in. Was she a friend of Daphne's? A long-lost relative? Instinct told her that this was the photo missing from the album she and Daphne had been looking at last week, the one that had made Daphne so shocked and secretive.

Downstairs again, Mel and Alice put away the cleaning gear and went their separate ways. Mel drove home with the photo in her bag, her mind full of ideas, images and possibilities.

CHAPTER FIVE

Directly after her lunch, Mel drove to the nursing home and asked to see Daphne. The photo of Rosa was in her bag, but she had no clear idea about whether to show it or not. All depended on Daphne's state of health.

'Melanie,' Daphne said and struggled to sit up in bed, her face pale but determined. 'How lovely to see you.'

Mel pulled a chair to the bedside.

'How are you, Daphne?'

'Still alive!'

A vivid smile broke through the tiredness.

'I haven't been lately because they said visitors would only tire you. But it's good to see you looking a bit better,' Mel said, smiling.

'Yes, I'm improving. But as for visitors tiring me—I should say so! That wretched James was here, bothering me, getting me to sign things.'

'What sort of things?'

Instantly, Mel was suspicious. How dare he come here and upset his aunt when all the advice had been to allow her to rest and recover?

'Oh, papers about my investments, mostly banking orders.'

Daphne shook her head and smiled.

'No need to look like that, my dear. After

all, he's only seeing to my finances for me, arranging the necessary fees for my being here. Good of him, really, considering how we've never got on, but I could have done without his chatter. Well, never mind, I must stop complaining, mustn't I?'

Mel laughed.

'Your complaints never last long, Daphne. You're an example to us all!'

'Now, tell me about the garden. How is it looking?'

Mel smiled, concentrating on the pictures in her head.

'Well, Susi is queen of the weeding and working really hard. And she's found your famous dragon plant. I know she wants to come and show it to you, but I thought another day, when you're stronger.'

'Susi can come whenever you can manage it, or perhaps Becky would bring her. They'd be very welcome.'

Daphne's smile was relaxed now and at once Mel was reminded of the photo in her bag. She tried to decide whether to take it out and show Daphne, but then decided not to. She recalled how its absence from the album had upset her, and now that she was so much weaker, it would surely be foolish to mention it again. So it remained in her bag as she changed the subject back to the garden.

'I've been tidying the border, deadheading the roses yet again, making room for the new seedlings that seem to be popping up everywhere.'

'Yes, the seedlings.'

Daphne had a faraway expression on her face, and Mel waited.

'I always let self-sown seedlings stay where they are, in moderation, of course. The new little love-in-the-mists and those pale Iceland poppies look lovely as other plants fade and die. Don't be too tidy with them, Melanie, will you? And what about the shrubs, and the herb garden? And, oh, dear, soon it'll be time to think about planting more bulbs for the spring.'

They looked at each other and Mel knew their thoughts were shared. Would Daphne still be here next spring? Mel's voice was husky as she said quickly, 'Don't worry, I'll see to it all, I promise you. I won't let your garden disappear.'

Daphne nodded and eased herself back on to the pillows. For a moment she was silent and then she said, 'Have you seen Stephen lately?'

With surprise, Mel watched an almost mischievous expression appear on her face.

'Is he being a good neighbour?' Daphne continued. 'What's your opinion of him, my dear?'

Mel was amused at this sudden change of mood, but not quite certain how to answer all the questions. She decided to take them in turn, and she certainly wouldn't say anything about sharing fish and chips by the river.

'I saw him the evening he moved in,' she told Daphne. 'He's a quiet neighbour and not a nuisance, even though he did run short of milk and came bothering me.'

She stopped. Daphne was still smiling, but Mel felt she was being put to the test. How obvious it was now that dear old Daphne was matchmaking! She decided to laugh it off.

'And I think he's a nice guy, but you know me, Daphne. I'm too busy to bother with men these days!'

The perceptive eyes regarded her steadily and for a moment Mel heard the hollowness in her defiant words. Yes, Stephen was nice, and yes, she liked him enormously, what she knew of him. Suddenly her memories of herself and Andrew were changing. After all, they had both been so young, hardly realising the commitment of marriage. She even wondered if the split up might have been partly her fault.

'I see,' was all Daphne said, but Mel knew for certain that Daphne had guessed at the thoughts that raged through her just then. 'Well, my dear, you must live your life as you think fit, as I did.'

The awkward moment was past and Mel picked up the clue gratefully.

'Ever since I've known you you've been independent, Daphne.'

'And I still am. But sometimes—'

Suddenly the brilliant smile faded and a wistful note came into her weary voice.

'Sometimes I think how nice it would be to have had a family. Wouldn't you agree about that, my dear?'

Mel nodded. She certainly did. Automatically, her fingers went to her bag hooked on the back of the chair, and she took out the photo.

'Daphne, I found this at the back of your chest of drawers, covered with dust and cobwebs. I wasn't sure whether to bring it to you or not. It's the one missing from your album, isn't it?'

She laid the photo on the sheet and watched Daphne look down at it. Silence spread for an ever-lengthening moment and Mel could only guess at Daphne's reactions. She was staring at the photo, not smiling, not seeming to feel anything much, but then, abruptly, she lifted her head, looked into Mel's anxious eyes.

'Yes,' she said, 'you were right to bring it. It must have fallen when I was dusting one day. It's been missing for a long time.'

Another silence followed, and then she smiled, wearily, Mel thought, as if ending a long journey that had been tiring and emotional.

'I'd like you to show it to Stephen, please, Melanie. Will you do that for me?'

'Yes, of course I will. I'll see him this afternoon.'

She bit her lip. Better not to tell Daphne about James stealing the cottage key. Clearly she was ready for another rest, leaning back in the bed, eyes already half-closed.

Mel replaced her chair, picked up the photo and her bag and said quietly, 'I'll come again soon, Daphne.'

'Thank you. Goodbye, my dear.'

Mel left, seeing that her old friend was almost asleep before she closed the door.

Parking outside Glebe Cottage that afternoon, she saw two other cars, Stephen's and James's. She went into the garden and then stopped, hearing voices inside the cottage. Stephen hadn't asked her to be there, but Mel told herself she was the one who held the commission from Daphne and so she had every right to join him in confronting James. She entered the cottage and then paused, listening at the drawing-room door.

'I don't care a damn what she asked you to do, Summers, I'm her legal next of kin, so of course I needed the blasted key! Mel Brooks hasn't exactly been helpful either. But it was easy enough to take the key while she wasn't looking.'

Mel marched into the room.

'Thanks very much, James,' she snapped. 'Not helpful? So who persuaded Daphne to allow you to look at her investment portfolio? Who brought it into town for you? Well, let me tell you, next time you ask a favour, I won't be so willing to help out!'

The two men turned as she spoke. Despite looking at James's startled face, she thought she caught a quick glimpse of an approving grin from Stephen. Then James came towards her, his sudden smile a picture of wrongfully blamed innocence.

'Come on, Mel, love, don't be like that.'

Her voice rose as she rasped, 'I'm not your love and don't ever think it! Just keep out of my way from now on, James. I can understand how Daphne feels about you if this is how you behaved when you were younger.'

Suddenly his expression changed into anger and she stepped back.

'Oh, really? Give you all the details of my criminal past, has she? Then you won't be surprised if I tell you that I've been upstairs in the old girl's bedroom searching for something important. Seems you haven't quite got the intelligence, Mel, to understand that a solicitor acting for a client is perfectly within his rights to look for relevant documents!'

Stephen then spoke quietly, but with an authority that made them both turn to look at him.

'And did you find what you were looking for, upstairs, in Miss Chandler's bedroom?'

His disapproving tone of voice brought a look of frustration to James's face and Mel thought, thank goodness Stephen's here. He's bringing everything back under control.

'No,' James grated, striding towards the doorway, then turning and flinging the key on to the table near him. 'Here's the blasted key!'

He glared at Stephen, who passed the key to Mel.

'But don't think I won't get my way in the end! I'm her only living relative so I have the right to do whatever I want with her property.'

'Not until Miss Chandler is dead,' Stephen reminded him quietly. James's smile was unpleasant. He leered across the room.

'That what you think?' he snapped then marched out of the house.

Mel let out her tightly-held breath and went across to the window, making sure he'd gone. Not until she heard his car screech away did she turn and look questioningly at Stephen. He was standing quite motionless, staring up at a framed picture on the opposite wall, and the thought came to her that this stillness was part of his unusual attraction, that and his deep, low voice, and his ability to make sense of what seemed to her to be a painful muddle. As if he felt her eyes on him, he turned and smiled.

'You did well. I like a woman to speak out for herself. You got him right on the chin.'

'And so did you.'

Mel felt herself respond to his composure, flopping down in one of the chintzy armchairs. She laughed briefly.

'I almost feel sorry for him! Poor James!

What a tizz he was in. But what did he mean about not waiting for Daphne to die?' she added.

Casually, Stephen crossed the room and sat on the arm of her chair, looking down at her.

'Bluff, probably, but maybe he's got a surprise up his sleeve. These legal eagles know all the loops and ploys. Don't worry about it, Mel. He can't really do much harm, you know, despite all his blathering.'

'I suppose not.'

She felt she never wanted to move, sitting here with him so close, but a feeling of confusion forced her into action. Getting up, she walked to the doorway, putting necessary distance between them.

'If he's been upstairs, I think I'll just go and have a look, see if he's done any damage.'

She heard Stephen following her as she went up to Daphne's bedroom. Feeling the need to break the silence, she said, 'Alice Smith and I spring-cleaned yesterday.'

Then she recalled Daphne's words about the photo. All that fuss with James had put it out of her mind until this minute. In the room she stopped, was about to find the photo in her bag, when her eyes fell on the open bureau and she gasped.

'He's broken into it!'

Stephen went over to the bureau.

'No key.'

'No, I took it with me. I thought it best.'

'But it didn't stop him. Wonder if he found what he was looking for.' Stephen glanced back at her.

'I guess he was looking for family papers.'

Instinctively she knew. She nodded, her throat dry, and pulled the photo from her bag.

'This, I think, is what he wants, this photo of—'

She paused. The young face in the photo stared up at her and as their eyes met, Mel felt something inside her experiencing a change, an understanding.

Rosa was holding her baby as if he were a priceless treasure. She wasn't smiling, but looking almost defiant. Is that what motherhood did—made you strong, caring, selfless and determined? She wished, suddenly, with all her heart, that both Daphne and she could have had family and so experienced what the girl in the photo was so clearly showing. Stephen's low voice broke into her churning thoughts.

'May I see?'

Startled, she handed over the photo.

'Actually, Daphne asked me to show it to you. She didn't say why.'

'No, she wouldn't. Thanks for bringing it. I'll take good care of it now.'

Mel caught a quick breath. What had she expected?

'But who is it? Somebody called Rosa, and there's another name on the back that I can't read. Why are you keeping it?'

His eyes were on her, bright, but wary. Mel's words erupted without further thought as her need to know escalated.

'What exactly are you doing for Daphne, Stephen? Why are you here?'

He came near enough for her to see the crinkling lines around his brilliant eyes, to sense the smell of leather from his jacket and his own, musty fragrance. She held her breath and stared, willing him to reveal himself. For that moment she felt they were closer than they'd ever been, that this could be the step she longed for, that the interest they shared over Daphne and her problems would help to forge a stronger bond between them.

But slowly Stephen shook his head, put the photo into his pocket and said, 'Sorry, Mel. If Daphne didn't confide in you, then neither can I. Please don't be upset.'

It was too much to bear. If she hadn't swung away from him, going to the bureau and rifling around in the drawers to hide her dismay, she thought she might have either wept on his shoulder or dealt with him as she'd done with James, giving him a well-deserved piece of her mind.

The drawers of the bureau were disturbed, but how was she to know if anything was missing? Wearily, she accepted that James had got one over her and Stephen was his usual enigmatic self.

From the doorway he said, 'Sorry, but I can't stay any longer. I've got an important date. Don't know when I'll be back. I really must go, Mel. Will you be OK here on your own?'

She turned around with a forced smile, thought he looked sincere in his apologies, but she wasn't ready to accept them. Her voice was sharp.

'Of course I will! If I can give James a fistful, I'll have no bothers with anything else, will I!'

She went back to the bureau, saying over her shoulder, 'Cheers then, Stephen. See you sometime, perhaps.'

She bent down to open the bottom drawer, hoping that his reply would at least offer a dreg of new hope, but he made no reply and she heard him going down the stairs, leaving her angry, sad and hopelessly confused about her own feelings.

* * *

Becky phoned when she got home after a short bout of gardening.

'Mel! Dreadful news!'

Mel caught her breath.

'What? Not Daphne? Oh, Becky, don't tell me!'

'No, no! She looked fine when Susi and I visited just now, but, Mel, that wretch James has done the dirty on her.'

'James? What's he done now?'

'Got her to sign a power of attorney form, that's what, so that he can now deal with all her belongings, including the cottage.'

'I don't believe it! Surely even James wouldn't force a sick, old woman to sign against her will.'

Becky guffawed down the phone.

'Nothing as obvious as that! Oh, no, our darling James has worked a real con trick on her. She didn't realise it until he sent her the copy of the signed paper today, telling her that from now on she wouldn't have to worry about a thing as he was going to deal with it all for her as she's given him power of attorney. The snake! How could he so such a thing?'

'Very easily.' Mel sighed. 'I suppose he just slipped the form in with the bank orders and investment forms she signed when she was feeling so poorly. She wouldn't have noticed, would she? Just one more form to put her name to.'

'I think you should go and see her, Mel,' Becky suggested. 'This must have been an awful shock. She seemed OK while we were there, and she had a great chat with Susi about her precious dragon plant, but I expect later, when she was alone, thinking about the cottage and what James would do, well, I don't know how she'll be feeling.'

'You're right. I'll go as soon as I can.

Thanks, Becky, for letting me know. See you tomorrow. Cheers.'

Rapidly, Mel dealt with mail that was urgent and then switched on the answerphone before she drove to the nursing home, her anxiety growing all the time. James's underhand action must have completely fazed Daphne. With the signed power of attorney form in his hands, of course he could now legally do whatever he liked with all her possessions. Mel went towards Daphne's room with rage glowing inside her.

Daphne sat up in bed, propped with pillows which nearly matched the pallor of her thin, lined face. She opened her eyes and looked at Mel for a long moment before speaking. Mel went to the bedside, pulling up a chair, looking into the shadowed grey eyes that watched her so intently.

'Daphne?' she ventured.

She was worried by the silence, by the brooding expression, and more than ever by Daphne's seeming lack of energy. But at last the silence was broken.

'Melanie.'

Slowly, wearily, Daphne lifted a hand and reached out. Mel took it between hers, gently stroking the bony fingers.

Wondering how to broach the subject she said carefully, 'Becky told me what James has done.'

It was difficult to know how far to go. She

94

didn't want to add to Daphne's obvious trauma, but felt that the awful business must be talked about.

'Yes,' Daphne said, and this time her voice was a degree louder. 'The wretch has been at his tricks once again.'

Mel watched with mounting surprise and relief as colour began to seep back into the pale cheeks. Suddenly Daphne's hand slid from her grasp and became a fist, thumping down on the duvet, startling Mel, making her sit back.

'But he won't get away with it this time! No, he certainly won't.'

Now Daphne sounded almost like her old, independent self. Her eyes, turned on Mel, were steely grey.

'Last time, he took money that I had in the house, but I couldn't prove he'd done it. Well, this time he's gone too far! I shall take him to court, sue him for false misrepresentation! Let's see how our charming young solicitor feels when he's the one being prosecuted!'

Mel stared, watching almost with disbelief as the weak old body who had seemed at death's door a few minutes ago had revived and become woman on the warpath. She met Daphne's determined smile with her own.

'That's wonderful! Of course you will, Daphne. I'm so thankful that you're taking it like this,' she said.

'The only other way is to give in to James

95

and I certainly refuse to do that.'

Mel watched admiringly and wondered if James realised what a feisty opponent he had in his aunt. Wryly she thought he had a nasty shock coming but then she faced the facts. Who would act for Daphne in this proposed prosecution? What if it was already too late to do anything to stop James? He was a speedy worker, and he'd had a whole day in which to put schemes into action.

'I'll do all I can to help, Daphne. Whom do I contact, and ask to act on your behalf?' she asked.

'Stephen Summers, of course. He's the man who'll deal with all this.' Daphne's usually gentle voice was resolute.

'Stephen?'

'Yes. He comes from a legal background. He'll know what to do.'

'But Daphne, I don't understand.'

'My dear Melanie,' Daphne said briskly, 'you don't have to understand, just do as I ask. Tell him to come and see me, at once.'

'I'm afraid I can't. He's gone away.'

Mel felt helpless and also irritated that Daphne refused to confide in her. Daphne frowned impatiently.

'Well, telephone him. Tell him it's urgent. He'll have to come back. Oh, yes, of course, I remember now. He told me he was going. So maybe we'll just have to leave things until he returns.'

Mel blinked. She wished someone would enlighten her.

'Do you know when that'll be?'

Daphne gazed at her for a moment and then shook her head.

'It all depends,' she said slowly, and then dropped back on her pillows. She closed her eyes and Mel's anxiety flew back again.

'Daphne, are you all right?'

'Yes, my dear, just a bit tired. I think I'll rest now.'

'Of course. I'll go. Good-night, Daphne. I'll see you tomorrow.'

Mel crept out of the room, her mind a whirl of images and thoughts which seemed impossible to piece into an understandable whole. All she knew for certain was that James was now in control of things, and that Stephen had disappeared just when he was so desperately needed.

Something drew her to Glebe Cottage as she drove home. Perhaps it was the knowledge that, unless legal action could be taken against him, James would undoubtedly put it up for sale. That would mean the end of Daphne's beloved paradise garden.

Mel went through the gate and up the path, looking around her with new vision. Yes, it was much tidier now, and some of the new summer seedlings were flowering. She and Susi, and Becky, too, had done a good job to restore the garden to some of its past glory. But for how much longer would it look like this? She shut her eyes quickly, to blot out imaginary visions of future owners of the cottage either turfing the whole garden, or filling it with the trendy decking and entertainment areas as seen on television. Then she told herself to be sensible. Daphne was relying on Stephen and so must she. There was, after all, nothing else she could do.

She wandered around, seeing what more needed to be done here. Tomorrow, after seeing Daphne, she would muster Susi and Becky again and together they would carry on the good work. Feeling slightly less doleful, Mel returned to her car, only to be hailed by Julia Wells, walking briskly towards the vicarage.

'Hi, Mel! I've been meaning to ring you all day. I've remembered where I saw the name of your new neighbour, Stephen Summers.'

Julia hesitated tantalisingly and Mel, wishing she were elsewhere, said coolly, 'Oh, yes?'

'On the telly, that's where! Must have been last winter. He was presenting a programme on researching family trees. I remember watching because we were interested in finding out about our own.'

Mel locked her car and turned, staring into Julia's smiling face. 'A television presenter? Stephen?'

She wasn't sure if she was shocked or

pleased, or just plain amused.

'Oh, no,' Julia said quickly, 'not just a presenter. Apparently he's a really famous genealogist. I read an article about him. He's freelancing now. Lost his wife some time ago in a car crash, poor man. We must try and make him feel at home here.'

'He's not staying much longer,' Mel said shortly, trying to control her distaste of all this publicity. 'Said he was looking for a permanent home somewhere.'

That wasn't precisely what Stephen had said, but perhaps it would stop the village gossip which seemed to be centred on him at the moment.

'Sorry, Julia, I'm in a bit of a rush.'

She turned away. Now her mind buzzed. A genealogist? No wonder, then, that he had a copy of the Chandler family tree. So that was the little job Daphne had entrusted him with, searching out her own tree. And to what end? Suddenly Rosa and her baby flew into Mel's thoughts—another forgotten branch? But surely, if so, Daphne would have mentioned them at some point in the last few years.

And then came the all-important question—how to get hold of Stephen when she had neither address nor phone number. It was very well for Daphne to issue orders like that. Mel had to grin as she recalled the fighting gleam in those grey eyes. But there was no way she could comply, simply wait until he chose to contact her, if he ever did.

As no resolutions appeared to all these complexities, she knew she must live with the situation and not let it overload her. She needed to take her mind off things, so when she got home, she called Becky, knowing she badly needed a friendly voice and the familiar support that had always been there in the past.

'Becky? Thought you'd like to know that Daphne's taken it on the chin, about James and his double-dealing. She's threatening to take him to court, would you believe?'

'Good for her! So there's plenty of life in the old girl yet! Marvellous news, Mel. Hey, why don't you come round for supper? I'm just trying out a recipe. Are you on?'

'I'd love to come. Thanks. I'll be around soon. 'Bye.'

Thank goodness for friends and understanding, Mel thought as she went into her work room and dealt with the paperwork awaiting her, and that in itself helped clear her mind of uncertainties and lost hopes. Later, spruced up, she drove round to Becky's house, intent on having an enjoyable evening away from all the trouble and worry over Daphne.

The game pie Becky had concocted was excellent and would definitely be scheduled for future menus. Later, sitting outside on the small, flower-laden terrace with coffee and brandy, Mel felt relaxed. But still she couldn't quite rid herself of the knowledge that she should be trying to work out a way of doing as Daphne had asked.

Becky was watching her, and said at last, 'OK, out with it. You're sitting there fidgeting with your brandy glass as if it were worry beads. What's bugging you?'

Mel laughed.

'Psychic, are you? But then it's not the first time you've seen through my amazing façade of calmness and serenity. You picked me up from the floor several times after Andrew and I split, as I remember. Becky, I need to get in touch with Stephen. Like I said just now, Daphne said go and do it. I told her I don't know where the wretched man is, but that didn't stop her orders coming thick and fast.'

'Is that all?'

Becky let out her familiar loud, jolly laugh and got up, going towards the telephone and producing a bunch of scribbled notes.

'It's somewhere here. Let's see.'

Mel sat up.

'What is? Don't tell me you've actually got his number.'

'Hang on. Surely I didn't bin it, did I? Could've done. Susi keeps coming in with all these bits and pieces.'

Becky scrabbled furiously.

'What's Susi got to do with Stephen's number?'

'Oh, he gave it to her. Said to ring him if she had any more problems with the herbs and the

101

magic.'

Becky threw a wide grin over her shoulder.

'Nice guy, isn't he? Should have kids of his own.'

'Maybe he has.'

Mel felt her spirits take an unwanted downward dive, but Becky was putting a crumpled piece of paper in her hand.

'Here you are, his mobile number. Go on then, ring him. I'll go into the garden and converse with the water butt while you talk. Never think I'm one for gossip.'

Picking up her glass, she left the terrace, heading down the garden, only pausing for a last snipe over her shoulder.

'Get on with it, Mel, for heaven's sake. I can't stand all this angst much longer, and give him my love. If you don't want him, I do.'

Mel laughed a little self-consciously, but took the paper to the phone and keyed in the number. She wasn't sure what she would say, or how he would react, but this was what Daphne had asked her to do, and so she must just get on and do it.

She waited, listening to the phone ringing, and ringing, and ringing . . .

CHAPTER SIX

At last, after a seemingly endless delay, during which Mel's spirits plummeted even further, she heard the familiar low, gravelly voice. 'Stephen Summers.'

Catching her breath, excitement rushing through her, she tried to remember what she needed to say.

'It's Mel. Sorry to be a nuisance.'

What was she talking about? This was ridiculous. 'I mean, I know it's late—'

Even worse! She wondered if she shouldn't just hang up and creep away. Where was the Mel who had put James in his place so satisfyingly? Rage and embarrassment filled her.

'You could never be a nuisance, Mel,' Stephen soothed. 'Something wrong?'

She might have known he'd understand.

Thankfully she said, 'Stephen, James has played a cruel trick on Daphne and she's asked me—ordered me, actually, to find you. She said you're the one who can deal with it. Becky gave me your number.'

'I see. What's he done?'

Mel sighed with relief and told him what Daphne had said.

She couldn't help adding, 'What a snake James is! Daphne's an old lady and shouldn't have to take all this hassle.'

'I agree, but she's also quite tough. Don't worry, Mel, I'm sure I can sort things out.'

'But how? You're not here.'

Again Mel began to feel the old irritation, the sense of being shut out while inexplicable things happened around her.

'That's very true. And who knows where I'll be tomorrow? Sorry, Mel, but I can't really say. So much going on at the moment.'

'What is going on?' she almost shouted, but as usual he steered her off course.

'Don't get so het up. You'll lose your beauty sleep if you go to bed in this state.'

She heard the amusement in his voice but wasn't amused.

'Of course I'm het up! You go off to goodness knows where and—'

'Susi knew, too. You've managed to find me, haven't you?'

The final straw, that was, and Becky was back on the terrace, smiling questioningly, no doubt expecting a happy ending to the conversation.

Mel said sharply. 'And I'm sorry I did. Well, at least you've got the message. It's all up to you now. I've done my bit. Good-night, Stephen.'

She didn't wait for his reply but slammed down the handset, then stared at Becky miserably.

'I'm going home and I think I'll have a

double Scotch before I go to bed. And what are you grinning at, you wretch?'

Becky gave her a hug and said comfortingly, 'Sorry, but you and your muddled thinking really make me laugh.'

Mel walked towards the front door and then stopped. She turned.

'Explain. Muddled thinking? I don't know what you mean.'

'Yes, you do. *Who Needs Men? Not Me!* has suddenly been pushed aside by *I Need a Man and Stephen Could Be That Man.* Agreed?'

Becky's smile was warm and understanding. Mel stood very still, thoughts dancing through her mind. At first she was ready to snap off Becky's head but slowly the truth—unwanted truth—blanked out all the anger and hurt dignity that had shored her up since Andrew and she parted.

'Agreed,' she said grudgingly, and refused to look at the approval on Becky's face. She hesitated, and then added, 'But don't go on about it. I could still be wrong. I mean, what's the point of wanting a guy when he clearly doesn't want me?'

And then, perhaps because she didn't want to hear Becky's response, she rushed on.

'I didn't tell you. Julia Wells has remembered that she saw Stephen on TV, presenting a programme about researching family trees. Apparently he's a famous genealogist.'

Becky gasped.

'So that explains why he's here—finding out about Daphne's non-existent family? Has he said anything to you about it?'

'No. Keeps changing the subject when I try to ask. But I did see a copy of the Chandler family tree on his table.'

'This is getting really exciting! Hey, what if he comes up with Daphne's long-lost lover, the guy in the photo you told me about?'

Mel considered this.

'Could be, but why is Stephen so secretive about it all? It's as if he didn't trust me.'

'Ah,' Becky said wisely. 'Trust, the difficult bit. And that brings us back to you, Mel.'

'What do you mean?'

Mel stood in the doorway, caught by the sudden seriousness in Becky's voice.

'Look, you think you've fallen for Stephen, which means that you know a bit about him.'

'But I don't, except what Julia told me.'

'Right. Let's put it another way. You like what you don't know.'

'Becky, shut up. I'm going home.'

'I'll shut up when I've finished. OK, you love him, but you don't trust him. There's something wrong somewhere.'

Becky came towards her, giving her another hug and smiling in the old, affectionate way. Mel's emotions suddenly hit her and she wanted to let out all the feelings that churned away inside. She went quickly through the house towards the front door with Becky behind her.

'Trust, like I said. Sleep on it, girl.'

Becky's voice followed Mel as she turned, smiled, said, 'OK, I'll do my best. Thanks, Becky,' and left the house.

After lunch next day, Mel worked hard in the paradise garden, and was joined by Becky and Susi when school came out.

'Lovely, isn't it?' Becky said, strolling down the path admiring the colours and scents of the plants that lined the wide border.

Mel straightened up from tying back straying tendrils of everlasting white sweetpeas.

'Better than it was.'

She surveyed her work and knew, with a sudden pang of joy, that the garden did, indeed, look more like itself. Daphne, she thought, would be pleased. If only they could bring her here to see it.

'It's so quiet.'

Becky watched Susi communing with the herb garden and grinned over her head at Mel.

'Peaceful. No bad thoughts here. I suppose that's what Daphne misses more than anything else. Serenity.'

Mel nodded, sharing the calming thought.

'Yes, you're right. I wonder if . . .'

But she got no further. Something was chugging noisily along the road, stopping outside the garden gate. Becky sucked in a disbelieving breath.

'Good grief! It's a digger. What on earth is going on?'

Mel ran to the gate to see a man climbing down from the cab and approaching her. He nodded.

'Glebe Cottage? Mr Chandler here?'

'No,' Mel grated. 'Is he supposed to be?'

'Said he'd show me which fence to take down to get the machine in.'

Mel stared at the man. For a moment she thought she must be hallucinating. James obviously meant to dig up the garden! And what then? Probably make it into one of those trendy television showpieces, all decking and paving. She exploded.

'No! There's no question of you coming into this garden. It's private property. Just clear off.'

The man frowned.

'Hold on, Mr Chandler said—'

'I don't care what he said!'

But suddenly the truth hit her. With power of attorney over Daphne's possessions, James could do exactly what he wanted to do, and Glebe Cottage was the first thing to be dealt with. He'd sell it, make money, assure Daphne that her fees at the nursing home were adequately provided for, and probably pay himself a backhander for arranging things so well, if she knew James.

By now, Becky was at her side, with Susi

running towards the gate from the herb garden, a small piece of the dragon plant in her hand.

'What's happening?'

In a few curt words, Mel explained the horrific situation.

'Oh, no,' Becky said, 'he can't do that,' and Susi's high voice chimed in, 'It's a dragon, isn't it, Mum? That horrid yellow thing out there. Oh, don't let it come in!'

Mel's mind had stopped igniting flames of disgust and horror. Now she was cool and ready to fight. She smiled at the gaping man outside the gate.

'I'll give Mr Chandler a ring and sort this out. Just wait, will you?' she said.

'Sure.'

He nodded resignedly and looked over her shoulder.

'Lovely garden,' he said amicably. 'Pity to dig it up, eh?'

Mel found her mobile and phoned James.

'James is out this afternoon. Can you leave a message?' the receptionist asked.

Mel snorted and slammed down the handset.

'He's on his way,' she told Becky grimly. 'Any minute now.'

It was, in fact, ten minutes later when James's car did appear outside and he came into the garden, smiling and patting Susi on the head.

'Hi, Mel. Glad you're here. This chap's come to let you off any more of this hard work. I'm putting it down to gravel. Easy to handle, and attractive when the estate agents come to photograph the old place.'

Mel met him by the bench and forced herself to return his smile.

'No, you're not, James,' she told him lightly. 'I'm not going to let you do anything so horrific to Daphne's beautiful garden. I don't care if you think you've got the legal right to do so. Yes, I know about the way you conned her into signing a power of attorney form, and I'm prepared to fight you all the way, through the courts, if necessary, to prove what an illegal action that was.'

They stared at each other and she added slowly and deliberately, expanding her smile so that the insult hit home with even stronger impact, 'You're a liar and a cheat, James Chandler, and I never want to see you again.'

James switched on his charming smile.

'Wonderful! I really do like a woman who speaks her mind, but look, Mel, it's not what you think. Daphne knew what she was signing. I mean, she's a poor old thing with a muddled mind, but I told her what it was, and of course she was only too pleased to let me take everything off her shoulders.'

Beside Mel, Becky said angrily. 'Absolute nonsense! Daphne herself told me that you'd conned her. I saw her yesterday afternoon and she was as bright as a button and extremely angry. What a snake you are, James.'

Mel thought this unpleasant discourse might well turn into a real brawl, so interrupted forcefully.

'No way will I let you take down a fence and trespass on Daphne's garden, so just push off, James, and take that wretched contraption with you.'

At her side, Susi suddenly piped up.

'Here's the dragon plant!'

She held up a piece of tarragon and thrust it towards James's face. He stepped back crossly.

'What on earth?'

'This'll get rid of your dragon, see if it doesn't. It's magic, and it'll kill your beastly old dragon!'

Mel hesitated. This was no place for a child at the moment. She glanced at Becky, who nodded, took Susi's hand and led her away, talking quietly to her and explaining that it was time to go home. No doubt the dragon would be gone by tomorrow.

James was laughing loudly.

'Magic! Dragons! What's going on here?'

Then a car drew up outside the gate and he turned, craning his head.

'Who's this? Could be the guy from the estate agents.'

But it was Stephen! Mel's anger changed into delight. She watched him look at the digger, have a word with the driver, nod his head, and then come into the garden.

'Mel,' he said, with a flash of brilliant smile. 'And Becky, Susi.'

For a moment he laid his hand on the child's shoulder, and she looked up at him.

'Are you going to kill the dragon, Stephen?' she asked, eyes alight with excitement.

'Yes,' Stephen said, 'with your magic help, Susi. But I think you'd better move back, in case there's a real fight.'

He nodded at Becky, who took up the cue, stationing herself and Susi by the cottage door. Stephen looked at James.

'You haven't got a leg to stand on, Chandler,' he said matter of factly.

James blustered.

'What do you know about it? Keep out of this. It's nothing to do with you.'

'Wrong,' Stephen said, with a wry grin. 'I've got everything to do with it.'

James stared with furious eyes but Stephen stepped past him, reached the bench and sat down, pulling papers from his pocket.

'Let me explain,' he said, patting the seat beside him. 'It won't take long.'

Like a small boy in the headmaster's study, James reluctantly obeyed. Fascinated, Mel watched. Stephen had come back after all, was here at just the right time, and seemed to think he could tip James's plans into space. Her mind whirled. She waited impatiently while he sorted out a particular paper and passed it

112

over to James.

'This is a copy of the Chandler family tree. Your aunt has commissioned me to work on it, as I'm a genealogist. She believes she has other relatives, despite what she's always told the family.'

James looked uncomfortable.

'I don't believe it.'

Shrugging his shoulders, Stephen said, 'That's what everyone says when something unthought-of turns up. Believe me, I have proof that you are definitely not the only relative alive at this time.'

'But I'm still next of kin.'

'Afraid not. You see, your aunt had a secret relationship and was actually engaged to a Major Phillip Wright just before the end of the Second World War, but he was killed in action. The child of that union, Rosa—'

Mel gasped, and for the first time Stephen looked up, smiled at her again and said to James, 'Move up, Chandler. I want Mel to share in all this.'

Sitting beside him, Mel could only stare at the paper he put on her lap. There it was, the birth certificate of Rosa Chandler. She said nothing, but the confusion grew. James, on the other hand, was scornful.

'You chaps are all the same, worming out secrets. The family knew that something funny had been going on in Daphne's life, but she chose not to tell. My mother used to hint at it, and I don't see that having a birth certificate can change anything except bring her sordid little affair into the open.'

'It changes everything,' Stephen told him sharply. 'Above all, you are no longer her next of kin.'

'Rubbish! This girl, Rosa, never did a thing for her, just went off and disappeared. But I've looked after my aunt and right now I'm legally managing her affairs.'

'Illegally.'

Stephen turned, looked James in the eye and Mel winced. She knew that look.

'Getting your aunt to sign that form without knowing what she did is illegal. I intend taking steps on her behalf to sue you for the action.'

Mel watched James's expression change from indignant certainty to sudden insecurity. He said nothing but got up, pacing the garden path. Stephen followed him.

'You'll be hearing from Miss Chandler's new legal adviser very soon. Take my word, you'll find it hard to get out of this. Now, I think you should go, and take that yellow monster with you. There are no fences coming down in this garden, not ever.'

They all watched as James shouted some furious words to the machine driver and then got into his car and roared away.

Stephen turned to Mel.

'I'd love a cup of tea. I've driven from Wales and I'm exhausted.'

114

He grinned, then put an arm around her shoulders and kissed the cheek nearest to him.

They all drank tea, Becky and Mel sitting at the kitchen table in Daphne's kitchen with Susi standing close to Stephen, on the opposite side. Magic was under discussion, and Susi was radiantly describing to Stephen exactly how she, and the magic plant, had managed to kill the awful yellow dragon. Stephen smiled into her excited face.

'And I'll tell you something else, Susi. There's more magic to come, probably next week, or soon after.'

'What is it?'

He cocked an eyebrow over the table, gave Mel the usual flash of a vivid smile, and looked back at Susi.

'It's a secret. Can't tell you, not yet, but keep up your magic work, Susi, won't you?'

'Next week! Oh, yes, I will. Mum, did you hear that? More magic next week!'

Later, after Becky and Susi had gone home, Mel walked around the garden beside Stephen. He had taken her hand and she felt his warmth and strength as a blessing, something she knew now that she'd missed ever since she and Andrew parted. And instinct told her that this particular blessing was going to last, if only Stephen would suggest that it might. But would he? Enigmatic as usual, he was talking of disappearing yet again. She forced herself to keep calm, despite the disappointment surging through her.

'A few more bits to piece together, Mel. That's why I must go.'

'Where to?'

But she knew he wouldn't tell her. He was a man of integrity.

'Not far away, and then I'm going to see a cousin of mine and get him to deal with James Chandler and his fraudulent ways.'

He looked down at her as they sat on the bench beneath the honeysuckle arch.

'You're very quiet.'

'Yes.'

She kept her head turned away. Don't let him see how I feel. Why can't he confide in me? Surely the business of researching Daphne's family tree and finding Rosa was finished. There could be no secrets left. And then the awful thought came—was she really sure Stephen was the man for her?

'What's the matter, Mel? Can't you tell me?'

'Why should I? You don't tell me anything.'

The words erupted before she could stop them, but she was glad they were out. If she and Stephen were to have a real relationship, honesty was all-important. He took both her hands in his and was silent. She knew he was waiting for her to turn and meet his eyes, but it took a little while of thought before she was able to do so. Then he smiled, slow and understanding, and she hoped with all her

116

heart that she hadn't spoiled things.

'I know how you must feel, sweetheart, but I can only ask you to wait a bit longer. The secrets aren't mine and I've still got things to do, people to see. It all takes time, but then I'll be able to concentrate on my own life.'

She nodded, her hands feeling warm and strengthened within his own. Sweetheart, he'd just called her.

He paused, then said, 'And perhaps on your life, Mel? Our life together?'

A delirious feeling of hope surged through her and at once she lifted her face to his. His lips were warm and loving, his response ardent, but too soon he drew away, returned her hands to her lap and stood up.

'I have to go, Mel. I don't want to, but—'

He shrugged and again she felt the cold thrust of anxiety unsettling her.

'Wait for the magic,' he told her, smiling, and then walked away down the path. At the gate he turned, looked at her for a long moment, and said, 'Trust me, sweetheart,' before going out to his parked car and driving away.

*   *   *

It was hard during the next few days to keep in mind those important words, trust me, but Mel concentrated on them. Thankfully she was kept occupied with the business, with finishing the cleaning of Glebe Cottage and still working in the garden most afternoons. But one thing cheered her. Visiting Daphne during the week she found her improving fast.

'Daphne, you look much better.'

She kissed the pale cheek and was thankful to see the grey eyes looking bright and energetic.

'I am, Melanie, very much better indeed. Stephen has written to tell me that James's wicked action of getting me to sign that form is now in legal hands, the best, he says, and there's no reason for me to worry about the young villain any more.'

She watched as Mel drew up a chair.

'And so Stephen is away again.'

'Yes.'

Mel looked down. She wasn't ready to show her feelings, just in case he didn't come back, in case the secrets took him somewhere else, in case that brief kiss had meant goodbye.

'Well,' Daphne said, sounding disappointed but amused at the same time, 'I expect he'll turn up again, like the proverbial bad penny.'

Mel smiled carefully.

'Perhaps. Just have to wait and see, won't we?'

And now it was over a week since he'd gone. The weather had turned dull and thundery, rain had fallen, so Mel had tied up the floppy bushes and overgrown perennials in the border in case another deluge descended. She was there on the Tuesday afternoon, glad that the cottage was once again shining and dust-free and that the garden, in the sunny aftermath of the storm, looked quite beautiful, for all it was late summer.

Alice Smith came outside. Mel stood up from bending and saw something different about her. Excitement?

'Are you off now, Alice?' she asked. 'Thanks so much for all your help. I told Daphne how hard you'd been working and she was delighted. Said to give you her very grateful thanks.'

'I know, Mel,' Alice said, with a big smile. 'She phoned me.'

'Did she? She really is feeling better, then.'

Mel was pleased with the way her old friend seemed to be regaining her lost health and energy.

'You just wait and see how much better!'

Alice went indoors again, which was strange as she'd already spent the morning in the cottage. Mel frowned. Then Becky and Susi arrived, grinning like a couple of lottery winners. Susi rushed up.

'It's the magic day!'

Becky said quickly, 'Susi, you're not to spoil things. Mel doesn't know.'

'Doesn't know what?'

Mel spun round and caught the wicked grin on her friend's face.

'What are you up to, you and Alice? What's

going on, for goodness' sake? And why haven't I been told?'

'Cool down, Mel. Just hang on and wait a bit longer. Ten minutes and then it'll happen.'

Mel felt the atmosphere begin to sizzle. Something strange was going on, but why should Alice, Becky and Susi know, and not her? Not another of Stephen's secrets, was it?

Then she started to smile. If it was, it had all the feelings of a happy secret. She put away her gardening tools, went indoors to wash her hands and saw, with astonishment, that the kitchen table was laid with cucumber sandwiches, Becky's famous Victoria sponge cake, scones, jam and a huge dish of clotted cream. She looked accusingly at Alice, busily getting out the best china and filling kettles.

'You know all about this, obviously, Alice. Who told you?'

'Stephen did, Mel. Rang me at home and said would I help Becky lay on a good tea this afternoon.'

Mel said nothing, but her mind raced in several directions at once, resulting in complete confusion. She decided to go and sit in the garden and await developments. Five minutes later a car drew up, driven by the matron from the nursing home. She smiled over the gate as she went to the boot and unfolded a wheel-chair.

'Miss Chandler will need a hand, please, Mel.'

Amazed, Mel felt her emotions start to rise, but she went to the car and helped Daphne out of the front seat. The grey eyes met hers with a new light of happy expectancy.

'Well, here I am, Melanie. All ready for the tea party.'

'So lovely to see you here, Daphne.'

Mel said no more, but wheeled the chair in through the gateway and up the garden path.

'Stop, please,' Daphne said, with a sudden tremor in her voice. 'Just let me look.'

Becky and Susi sat on the bench watching, with Alice standing in the open doorway of the cottage. Mel caught matron's smile, as she thought she had never known such a wonderful moment. Who would have thought Daphne would ever be here, in her beloved paradise garden again? Then the spell broke. Daphne asked sharp questions about various plants, and Susi came running to her side, offering a bunch of herbs and chattering on about magic. Mel watched Daphne's eyes turn to the child and smile, quickly forgetting her garden as she listened to Susi's thrilling explanation of how the dragon was defeated.

'And Stephen says there's more magic to come, Miss Chandler. I don't know when, but quite soon.'

'Really, Susi? Even more magic? In my garden? How exciting! I hope we don't have to wait too long.'

Becky was at her side, looking down the

path.

'Actually, I've got a feeling it's about to happen, Daphne. This must be Stephen now.'

Mel stood quite still as a car parked, and voices sounded. She was suddenly quite, quite sure that she loved Stephen, secretive as he was being, and it dawned on her that Becky's advice, together with his own words, trust me, had worked, giving her this wonderful knowledge of his love and her own returning feelings. She smiled, and waited for what might happen next.

Into the garden came a young woman, followed by a man of the same thirty-plus age group. Stephen closed the gate behind them, and instantly his eyes went to Mel. She caught his smile, delighting in the assurance in his loving eyes, and knew that all was well between them. Secrets might still abound, but no longer were they threatening ones.

She watched Stephen bend down and greet Daphne, saw him wheel the chair up the path and position it by the garden bench. He beckoned to Mel and to Becky and Susi, and then, looking back at the cottage, called to Alice to join them. Mel felt relaxed and elated. She didn't care what happened next. All that mattered was that Stephen was here and she knew that she loved and trusted him. And Daphne was here, too, but why was she looking up at the young couple with grey eyes shining, looking almost youthful herself?

Mel joined the little group by the bench, to hear Stephen introducing his companions.

'Daphne, this is your late daughter Rosa's son, Dominic.'

The photo flashed through Mel's mind. So Rosa had died, but Stephen had found her son, the baby she'd been holding. One of the secrets was now revealed.

'And this is Dominic's partner, Sarah. Dominic, this is Daphne Chandler, your grandmother.'

Mel turned away, instinctively allowing Daphne privacy to deal with this unexpected blessing of finding that, after all, she had a family, and a great-grandchild on the way, for clearly Sarah was pregnant. Mel took Alice and Becky into the cottage.

'Time to make the tea, I think,' she said, and they all smiled at each other.

Susi came rushing in.

'That was magic,' she shouted, eyes gleaming. 'Stephen's made Miss Chandler a grannie! Isn't he clever? And I'm clever, too, to have thought of using magic, aren't I?'

Becky hugged her daughter, then gave her a pat on the bottom.

'Yes, to all that, but don't get too cocky about it, love. Just go and wash your dirty paws before we start eating.'

It was an afternoon to remember. After tea, Daphne sat on the garden bench and talked to Dominic and Sarah. Mel and Becky were busy in the kitchen, clearing up, while Susi showed Stephen the results of her hard work in the herb bed, but it wasn't long before matron said it was time to take Daphne home. Mel looked at her old friend's glowing face and repeated the word.

'Home, Daphne?'

Just for a second, Daphne didn't answer and her eyes ranged around the garden and then back to the cottage. But she smiled resolutely.

'Yes, Melanie,' she said. 'The Grange is to be my home from now on, but when Dominic and Sarah—'

She looked up, reaching out her hand to touch Sarah's arm, and exchanging smiles.

'When they and the baby are living here they say I must come and visit. I can ask for nothing better.'

Mel nodded, her heart too full to reply. She watched Stephen and matron help Daphne into the car and then stood on the pavement close to Becky and Susi, with Dominic and Sarah beside them, waving as Daphne was driven off. Becky took Susi's hand.

'Bit of an anti-climax, isn't it, after all that excitement? But tomorrow's another day.'

'More magic?' Susi asked and her mother grinned.

'With you around, my cherub, who knows? Come on, time we went home, too. Can I give you a lift, Alice?'

Mel looked at Stephen as Becky drove off.

'And I suppose you have to go as well, as usual?'

But she smiled and he took her hands, looking down at her with an expression in his vivid eyes that made her heart sing.

'Right,' he said ruefully. 'I must drive Dominic and Sarah to the station to catch their train, and then I have to see about the matter of James Chandler. But I'll be back. Trust me, sweetheart.'

'I do,' she told him. 'But hurry back.'

She watched him drive away, knowing that there were still secrets between them, but trusting that soon they would all be revealed. However, she was wrong. Parking at Dunmore House she was startled to see an estate agent's sign at the gateway and even more amazed to read: SOLD.

How could it be? Surely the landlord should have told her? And was it being sold with her staying on as a sitting tenant? At least he couldn't kick her out. Again, anxiety wove around her milling thoughts. Indoors, she tried to phone the landlord but failed. Fuming, she sat and tried to be positive. What could she do at this late hour of day? Whom could she ask for advice? And why had Stephen disappeared, again? Momentarily her trust threatened to diminish, as a great muddle of worry washed through her. If only he were here. She realised again how much she desperately needed him, how deeply she loved him.

Her mobile rang as she went into the kitchen to fix herself a drink.

'It's all done, Mel,' Stephen said and his voice was cheerful. 'I'll be back soon. Fancy eating out?'

'Stephen!'

Laughter overcame the surprise. She might have known he'd be back, but even these short hours had seemed like years. She was about to tell him the news of the house being sold when he cut in.

'Hang on, Mel. I'm on my way. Wait till I see you. About fifteen minutes, OK?'

She shrugged.

'Right,' she said and then had to steel herself to wait all over again.

She was by the window in the front room when his car pulled up outside the house. Once in his arms, she kissed him fiercely.

'I love you, Stephen, but the house is sold and so I'm a bit het up, you see. I'll have to move out.'

She looked up into his eyes, wondering why he looked amused and not concerned. But then he drew her close, kissed her again before turning her to look at the house behind them.

'I do hope you won't move, sweetheart, at least not too far.'

She heard his deep chuckle and held her breath.

'Not another secret, surely? Tell me,

126

what've you done now?'

He linked his arm through hers and led her into the wilderness that was the back garden. Then he stopped, looking at her questioningly, as he spoke quietly.

'I've bought it, Mel. It's the sort of family house that I feel happy in. You see, I've been wandering for too long. Now I've found you, sweetheart, and the home where I want to live.'

She stared, uncertain where all this was leading.

'You mean, you downstairs and me upstairs? Is that it? But—'

She got no further.

'No buts,' he said quickly, 'and no separate flats either. I'm going to modernise the old place to the complete house it used to be, and will be again.'

Then he smiled and she waited, with expectancy soaring through her, for the rest of his plans. His voice was low, and she heard a note of uncertainty.

'I'm asking you to share it with me, Mel, sweetheart, making it into a family home.'

He put his hands to her face, lifting it to his, and kissing her with such abandon that for that brief moment Mel couldn't think straight. But he hadn't finished.

'There's a condition, of course,' Stephen added, looking away from her, but not before she saw the wicked twinkle in his eyes. 'I want you to make us a real garden here. You've got the knowledge and the experience now, and so I shall expect—'

She didn't let him finish.

'A paradise garden of our own, Stephen? But only if you help me with the paradise bit.'

Once more she was pulled into his arms.

'No problem with that,' he whispered, and kissed her in a way that made his promise come true.

We hope you have enjoyed this Large Print book. Other Chivers Press or Thorndike Press Large Print books are available at your library or directly from the publishers.

For more information about current and forthcoming titles, please call or write, without obligation, to:

Chivers Large Print
published by BBC Audiobooks Ltd
St James House, The Square
Lower Bristol Road
Bath BA2 3SB
UK
email: bbcaudiobooks@bbc.co.uk
www.bbcaudiobooks.co.uk

OR

Thorndike Press
295 Kennedy Memorial Drive
Waterville
Maine 04901
USA
www.gale.com/thorndike
www.gale.com/wheeler

All our Large Print titles are designed for easy reading, and all our books are made to last.